A Candlelight Ecstasy Romance®

"I'M TELLING YOU," HE CUT IN SHARPLY. "IF YOU LOVE ME, WITHDRAW YOUR APPLICATION."

"Is that a command?" Nicole asked heatedly.

"I loved you enough to give up a promising position just to be with you," he said in reply. "But you won't do the same for me. That tells me a hell of a lot about your love for me."

She didn't think she'd have to worry about her pounding heart anymore. It had stopped operating. "If you recall, I never asked you to make that grand sacrifice. In fact, I tried to talk you out of it. Had I known you'd throw it up to me, I'd never have let you ruin yourself on my behalf. Maybe we should have spared ourselves all this and split up then."

"Maybe we should have," Randell agreed curtly, and headed for the door.

By the time Nicole ran to the front window, his motorcycle was flying out of the parking lot. She put her forehead against the pane, wondering what she'd done.

CANDLELIGHT ECSTASY ROMANCES ®

194 A LASTING IMAGE, *Julia Howard*
195 RELUCTANT MERGER, *Alexis Hill Jordan*
196 GUARDIAN ANGEL, *Linda Randall Wisdom*
197 DESIGN FOR DESIRE, *Anna Hudson*
198 DOUBLE PLAY, *Natalie Stone*
199 SENSUOUS PERSUASION, *Eleanor Woods*
200 MIDNIGHT MEMORIES, *Emily Elliott*
201 DARING PROPOSAL, *Tate McKenna*
202 REACH FOR THE STARS, *Sara Jennings*
203 A CHARMING STRATEGY, *Cathie Linz*
204 AFTER THE LOVING, *Samantha Scott*
205 DANCE FOR TWO, *Kit Daley*
206 THE MAN WHO CAME TO STAY, *Margot Prince*
207 BRISTOL'S LAW, *Rose Marie Ferris*
208 PLAY TO WIN, *Shirley Hart*
209 DESIRABLE COMPROMISE, *Suzanne Sherrill*
210 LOVERS' KNOT, *Hayton Monteith*
211 TENDER JOURNEY, *Margaret Dobson*
212 ALL OUT TOMORROWS, *Lori Herter*
213 LOVER IN DISGUISE, *Gwen Fairfax*
214 TENDER DECEPTION, *Heather Graham*
215 MIDNIGHT MAGIC, *Barbara Andrews*
216 WINDS OF HEAVEN, *Karen Whittenburg*
217 ALL OR NOTHING, *Lori Copeland*
218 STORMY SURRENDER, *Jessica Massey*
219 MOMENT TO MOMENT, *Bonnie Drake*
220 A CLASSIC LOVE, *Jo Calloway*
221 A NIGHT IN THE FOREST, *Alysse Rasmussen*
222 SEDUCTIVE ILLUSION, *Joanne Bremer*
223 MORNING'S PROMISE, *Emily Elliott*
224 PASSIONATE PURSUIT, *Eleanor Woods*
225 ONLY FOR LOVE, *Tira Lacy*
226 SPECIAL DELIVERY, *Elaine Raco Chase*
227 BUSINESS BEFORE PLEASURE, *Alison Tyler*
228 LOVING BRAND, *Emma Bennett*
229 THE PERFECT TOUCH, *Tate McKenna*
230 HEAVEN'S EMBRACE, *Sheila Paulos*
231 KISS AND TELL, *Paula Hamilton*
232 WHEN OPPOSITES ATTRACT, *Candice Adams*
233 TROUBLE IN PARADISE, *Antoinette Hale*

A BETTER FATE

Prudence Martin

A CANDLELIGHT ECSTASY ROMANCE ®

Published by
Dell Publishing Co., Inc.
1 Dag Hammarskjold Plaza
New York, New York 10017

ISBN: 0-440-10520-X

Printed in the United States of America
First printing—May 1984

With grateful acknowledgment to
Barry Morris

To Our Readers:

We have been delighted with your enthusiastic response to Candlelight Ecstasy Romances ®, and we thank you for the interest you have shown in this exciting series.

In the upcoming months we will continue to present the distinctive sensuous love stories you have come to expect only from Ecstasy. We look forward to bringing you many more books from your favorite authors and also the very finest work from new authors of contemporary romantic fiction.

As always, we are striving to present the unique, absorbing love stories that you enjoy most—books that are more than ordinary romance.

Your suggestions and comments are always welcome. Please write to us at the address below.

Sincerely,

The Editors
Candlelight Romances
1 Dag Hammarskjold Plaza
New York, New York 10017

kisses are a better fate than wisdom.
—e. e. cummings

CHAPTER ONE

Nicole stirred. The sheet grazed her legs, crinkling with a soft whisper, a whisper that echoed the faint tremors chasing over her skin. Somewhere deep in her consciousness she felt the approach of her awakening. She resisted it. Though she usually greeted each morning eagerly, with the vigor and optimism of one well satisfied with her lot in life, this morning she was reluctant to wake. She wanted to linger within the dreamy cloud of sensation drifting through her sleep.

She sank into the pliant depths of her pillow, the damask, satin-slipped pillow she'd carried everywhere since first taking it to college a dozen years ago, and sank back into that nebulous but delightful haze.

A melting mist wafted over her nape, gently shifting the tousled array of her sable hair and teasing the shell of her ear. A warm cloak mantled the ridge of her spine, the curve of her buttocks. Tingles danced lightly beneath the touch of feathery fingertips swirling over her thigh. Insubstantial, lightly teasing, those fingertips edged their way into her slumbering senses, and Nicole quivered.

It was the sort of quiver she recognized, the sort only one man excited in her. She knew then she was dreaming of Rand. Of Rand, who could make her nerves hum with the melody of his love. She pressed her cheek deeper into the slick pinkish satin and delved deeper into her dream.

That gossamer touch inched upward, illusive and tantalizing. An incorporeal palm skimmed over the crescent of her hip, the airy fingers skated across the gentle swell of her stomach. Capricious, enticing, this dreamy hand was also beginning to torment.

Slowly, moving sluggishly within her veins, her blood started to simmer. She again shifted restlessly, then lay still.

The ethereal caress glided to the soft, dark tangle of curls between her thighs.

Desire wakened, rousing every nerve, every muscle, from the center of her being outward until her whole body tightened in response. An unconscious moan of pleasure flowed from her lips and Nicole parted her legs, inviting that spectral touch ever nearer.

A seductive massage answered her invitation. The calefacient simmer of her blood intensified and she awoke fully.

She lay coiled on her side, her body nestled intimately within the crook of his. Warm lips nuzzled the glossy, dark veil covering the nape of her neck. A solidly muscled chest pressed against the length of her supple spine. Smoothly textured thighs rubbed against the shapely satin of her own. Raspy wisps of hair grazed the contours of her calves. All this prodded her dormant perceptions, but none of this was responsible for her pulsating awakening. It was the arm, the hand, that prompted her to stir.

His left arm draped over her hip and across her stomach, burning a track on her skin to where his hand caressed her into moist submission. A heady fragrance wafted up to spur her into complete awareness. His exquisitely tender touch quickened her pulse and animated her nerve endings. She felt dewy and tingly and deliciously alive.

Opening her eyes, she saw the grayish tinge of dawn slipping in around the curtains, dimly illuminating the room, the bed. The bamboo-patterned sheet perfectly defined the outline of their bodies. The percale rustled slightly with his rhythmic motion. Her body rippled to the same cadence.

A muted incandescence shone within the darkened room. She slid her heavy-lidded gaze to the nightstand. The glowing green digits on the streamlined clock-radio were 5:11. Her half-formed gasp of pleasure was abruptly stifled, turning into a groan of censure. Five eleven in the morning! What was the matter with him?

She furrowed into the depths of her pillow. He burrowed into the arch of her neck. His tongue darted deftly over the increasingly unsteady point of her pulse. After a moment she sighed and turned her head, forcing him to pull away from her. She focused drowsily on his sensually full mouth.

A smile swaggered there, the sort of smile dripping with male satisfaction. It held a potent virility that momentarily mesmerized her.

"Ready on cue," he said, and the smile strutted on up to his eyes.

"It's a miscue . . . I'm not in this shot," she retorted.

The raspy texture of her voice belied her words. He listened only to that husky timbre. Watching the change in her expression, he slowly, seductively eased his fingers into the softness between her thighs. The cool metal of his ring sizzled against her heated flesh. His teasing touch renewed the force of her arousal.

But Nicole still resisted, some more prosaic part of her saying this was not the way to start a busy week. A dream was one thing, but this was altogether something else. Forty-five more minutes of sleep was what she needed. She attempted to elude the sensitive fingertips. Her attempt failed.

"Randell . . ." She sighed, half plea, half protest.

He answered the plea. He covered her mouth with his, thrusting his tongue between her lips without hesitancy. He swept his hands up over her belly and ribs to catch hold of her breasts with certainty. His kiss was firm and familiar, his touch was assured and arousing. He was like an artist bringing life to a canvas with masterly strokes he'd used a thousand times before. And what mastery he used! He knew just where to kiss, where to touch, where to most inflame her. Each light caress spread an aching, trembling warmth through her.

Whatever objection her mind might have, her body couldn't resist the rapturous yearning he summoned up so expertly. He evoked a need within her that had no thought for the time. Time had stopped. She rolled onto her back and gave herself up to the fulfillment of her dream.

His warm, deep chuckle caressed her lips. His softly spoken "Hold me" kissed her soul.

No longer capable of the least resistance, no longer wanting to resist, wanting only him, she responded to his soft request eagerly. She wreathed her arms about him.

reveling in the unique feel and scent and sight of him. Traces of dawn glinted like strands of topaz within the lustrous layers of his thick brown hair. Nicole's fingers itched to trap those strands, but she knew the amber in his hair was as elusive as the speckles of sunlight skipping over them. Instead, she spread her hands over his shoulders and pressed her fingers on the hard bone beneath the firm, smooth skin.

Rand kicked back the sheet and folded his body fully over hers. But he did not move to take her. He held himself immobile above her, gazing down at her, absorbing her feature by feature. His scrutiny stirred her as thoroughly as any caress. The dark shadow of desire within his eyes whet her appetite with a hunger only he could sate. She was swept up in his intensity. Her pulse pounded fiercely against her throat and her body clenched with need.

How was it, she dimly wondered, how was it he could still make her feel the urgency of the first time?

Something of her clamorous desire must have crossed her features, for a knowing smile gradually curved his lips. It softened the severity of his long, narrow face and indented twin grooves from the corners of his mouth to the edge of his chin. She reached up, drawn irresistibly to the crooked line of his smile. Lightly, almost imperceptibly, she brushed a fingertip over his lips. They both shuddered.

"You're so beautiful," he murmured, the force of his love deepening his resonant voice to a rough rasp.

His breath blew over her fingers. The warmth of it seemed to heat her soul, inflaming the brightly burning torch of her love. He was the spark that lighted the love within her. "It's you," she said breathlessly. "You make me beautiful. Always you. Only you."

With a low groan Randell bent to kiss her eyelids, the curve of her cheeks, the line of her nose. Finally, finally, he returned to her mouth and kissed her with such passionate fervor, she cried out. His name sang on the air between them.

She whispered his name over and over between the feverish kisses she randomly rained over his chin, his neck, the warm, firm skin of his shoulders and chest. Her hands moved urgently over his flesh, wanting him, needing him. She could feel the raging of his response in the sinuous flexing of the muscles beneath her fingertips, her lips as she traced each sleek, hard line of his body.

He cupped her breasts, skating his fingers along the soft undersides before sweeping up to palm her hardened nipples. He kissed the pink buds, then slid his mouth down her flesh until she whimpered deliriously. Her hair splayed in a dark fan over the pillow as she arched toward him. She closed her eyes and ears and knew only the ecstatic thrill of his hands and mouth, the intoxicating knowledge of what was to come. Her body quaked with expectation. Her blood steamed with anticipation.

She knew what he would feel like, hard and full within her. And she knew how she would feel, accepting him, becoming part of him. Knowing did not lessen the impact of her desire; it heightened the force of her excitement almost beyond bearing.

She ran her hands over him, feeling the shifting of the sinews in his shoulders, his back, his lean belly. She felt the hard swelling of his own desire grazing her thighs, and impatience overrode all else. If he didn't love her *now,* this instant, she would burst with the yearning.

"Take me, Rand . . . take me. . . ."

He lowered himself to her, but paused. Her eyes opened

and focused hazily on him. "I love you," he said, then thrust forward.

She gasped. A momentary satisfaction was deluged in a flood of overwhelming stimulation. She opened herself completely, welcoming the fulfillment, welcoming him. She watched the pleasure wash over his features as she automatically began to move with him. She watched his passion and love increase with their joining and gloried in them. Her own love expanded, filling every pore, every cell she possessed. The bed rocked with that love, ringing joyously in her ears, pealing *Randell, Randell, Randell.*

Soon she heard only her own faltering breath, her own irregular heartbeat. She was aware only of the driving force of his sex sinking into the moist cushion of hers. She locked herself about him and gave back the wondrous treasure she received.

Their union extended beyond the body, joining their spirits. It had always been thus for them. When she gave herself to Randell, Nicole always felt as if she were becoming part of him, as if they were one soul, one being, one spirit cherished beyond measure. And when he told her hoarsely that he loved her, she replied with a husky ardor that took him over the edge.

The tremor began in him, rippling tautly from his feet to the arch of his head. It ended in her, shaking her in the tension of release. They gripped one another and moaned in unison. Together they sank into triumphant oblivion.

Eventually Nicole realized the bed was no longer rocking, that she was no longer quaking. She was, in fact, almost no longer breathing. He stretched over her heavily, his weight crushing her slender frame. She grunted and shoved at his smooth chest. He raised up slightly, but didn't roll away. "Rand . . ." she groaned in a voice that clearly said, *Enough's enough.*

He grinned, the astoundingly boyish grin that had weakened more than one woman's knees over the years. It lighted his brown eyes with a glow that reflected the amber highlights of his hair and creased his generally somber face with lines that laughed. It invariably dazzled Nicole with a fresh realization of his masculine allure, and this time was no exception. He saw her open admiration and his smile softened. He tilted his head to the side and studied her quizzically.

"How is it, Mrs. Clarke," he finally asked, "that you manage to feel brand-new every time?"

"And how is it, Mr. Clarke," she returned pertly, "that you manage to make me feel that way every time?"

He chuckled softly and kissed the tip of her nose. "Not bad for nearly six years, eh, my love?"

"Well . . ." She drew out the word on a teasing roll.

"Don't tell me you have to think about it," he said, and his finely arched brows lifted.

"I think," she said with heavy emphasis, "that after almost six years you could've waited. Waking me up at five o'clock! You must be out of your mind, Rand."

"Can you think of a better way to wake?"

"Well, no," she admitted.

"There, you see? All I have to do is find a way to market it and alarm clocks will be as obsolete as sundials. We'll call it Clarke's Wondrous Waking Machine. Or maybe Marvelous. It was marvelous, wasn't it?"

"That's not the point," she insisted. "It wasn't *how* you woke me. It was *when* you woke me."

He sighed dramatically. "Six short years and the romance is dead. All she can think about is the time."

"And all he can think about is—"

A jangling clack was immediately followed by a mellow male voice stating that the skies were partly cloudy and the temperature was a chilly fifty-two. Nicole and Randell glanced at the clock-radio and moaned. They looked at each other and laughed. He slid off her, flopping onto his back, rubbed his hand down his chest, and commented idly, "It can't be all that chilly. I'm all sweaty."

"If you expect any sympathy," she said, "you've come to the wrong woman."

"Sorry to disagree with you, honey, but I most definitely came to the *right* woman."

She felt a rush of happiness, but merely rolled her eyes and said, "Go shower and let me get a few minutes deserved shut-eye."

"It's your turn to get up first."

"Not after you roused me from an utterly delightful dream—"

"I'd noticed you were somewhat roused. . . ."

The intimate husk in his tone brought an instant warmth to her skin, which he observed with blatant interest as it traveled from the high ridge of her cheeks to the firm swell of her small breasts. It never ceased to amaze her, the intensity of her reactions to him. Even after so many years, he held the ability to make her glow with just a word, a tone, a look. His continued fixed regard now darkened the heated flush to a deep scarlet and once again tautened the buds of her breasts. Slightly embarrassed as well as excited by this obvious evidence of his effect on her, Nicole slapped playfully at him.

He caught hold of her hand in midair and kissed the back of it. Sitting upright, he tugged on it. "Come on. Let's both get up and shower together."

"What's gotten into you?" she demanded. "A bushel of ginseng?"

He merely laughed and pulled on her hand. She allowed him to haul her from the bed and tow her down the hall. Watching the lean, long muscular line of his body as he strode down the shadowed passageway, she felt an inner pride radiate through her being. It was a body to stir any woman's blood, and it was a body she alone delighted in.

And how she delighted in it! Despite a togetherness that some people would have found smothering, she and Rand had never lost interest in the physical side of their marriage. Though not as frequent as it had once been, their lovemaking remained every bit as impassioned. It had, in fact, intensified. Each year the emotional bond between them had deepened, enhancing the impact of their physical loving. Like all couples, they'd had their problems, but never in bed. That was the one place where they always harmonized.

A satisfied smile touched her mouth. Yes, they knew how to make music in bed. As he'd said, not bad for nearly six years. She was still displaying that gratified smile of success when he dragged her into the bathroom.

Like the other rooms of their apartment, their bathroom was small but cleverly designed to make the most of the cramped space. Shelves above the tub and toilet, cupboards beneath the marbled sink, airy bright yellow walls, all seemed to expand the tiny square, but it was strictly an illusion. Like a well-choreographed dance team, they shuffled wordlessly around each other, avoiding elbows, fixtures, and walls. While Rand adjusted the heat of the water and the force of the spray, Nicole puttered with her usual first-thing-in-the-day routine. By the time she'd begun to brush her teeth, steam seeped into the air and fogged the mirror.

"Hey, beautiful, you'd better shake a leg," issued from behind the daisy-yellow shower curtain.

Beautiful. Nicole knew that the face behind the mist on the mirror wasn't beautiful. Having lived with that face for thirty years, she could easily enumerate all the defects —the pointed end to the chin she despairingly called her "witch's spike"; the too-small though admittedly well-shaped lips overshadowed by the too-long, too-thin nose; the high craggy ridge of cheekbones that kept her face from all claims of delicacy; the startling blue of her eyes, so pale that at times they appeared to be colorless, like translucent agates. Her shoulder-length hair was an unruly riot of black waves that refused to stay put for longer than ten minutes at a time.

Most detested of all were the thick black bars that sat heavily over her eyes. She hated those brows. They gave her face a severity she didn't feel suited her. When she was fourteen she'd taken her mother's razor and shaved them completely off, an action she'd lived to regret. They had grown in bushier than ever, annihilating her brief victory and condemning her to the lifetime chore of plucking them. But Randell, dear Randell, never even seemed to notice them. . . .

"Nicole, are you coming in or not?" asked dear Randell impatiently. He poked his head around the edge of the curtain. Froths of shampoo slithered down one ear and plopped onto his broad shoulder. His head disappeared and his disembodied voice added, "We'll be late if you don't start to hustle. The last thing we need on a Monday morning is to have the Lion snarling at us."

Mention of Lionel—known as "the Lion" by everyone

at the station for his fierce and frequent roars of dissatisfaction—spurred her to immediately join Rand in the tub. He stood directly beneath the shower nozzle, head flung back as he rinsed suds from his hair. Lather and water dripped in tantalizing tracks from his head to his shoulders, down his back and compact hips, to splatter onto the white porcelain. Nicole's eyes riveted on the sheer beauty of his sudsy body. She thought again how fortunate she was, to love and be loved by this man. Feeling invigorated with love and pride, she moved to share the water that splashed over his skin. She snuggled against him and pressed her palms flat on his wet chest.

He looked down at her and smiled. "It's about time, slowpoke. I was beginning to think you didn't want to shower with me after all."

"Actually, I didn't. You always hog the water."

"You should never," Rand said in misleadingly mild tones, "insult a man who holds the only bar of soap."

Before she could evade him, he slipped his arms tightly around her and energetically rubbed soap over her upturned face. She squealed, then sputtered as foam bubbled over the rim of her mouth. With a sudden twist, Rand reversed their positions and a full cascade of hot water drenched her face. Nicole gasped, choked, opened her eyes, and glared at him.

He gave her a look of choirboy innocence. "You'd better wash your hair, dear," he said in tones to match the look.

She flipped a finger in a rude gesture as she reached for the shampoo bottle, which he accepted with a laugh. She hadn't expected to get him angry. For one thing, such teasing was an integral part of their relationship. For another, it was as much an effort to get Randell angry as it was to demolish a mountain with a single firecracker. His makeup simply didn't include enough explosives to ignite a burst of temper. Which was, she thought as she vigorously applied shampoo to her scalp, a darn good thing, given the quick-fire powder keg of her own disposition. Her wrath, once provoked, was hot and venomous. With any other man, her temperament could have led to a volatile, unhappy situation; with Rand, it was like a balloon released unexpectedly. She'd start out with a loud blast, spin wildly with much noise, then deflate with a rapid fizzle. Rand simply wouldn't cooperate when she got mad. He'd wait patiently for her to calm down so they could talk things out, or—incredibly and highly irritating from her point of view—he'd do something to make her laugh and she'd be unable to continue storming.

It was, in fact, this ability of his to leash her tantrums that had first attracted her to him. Two years out of college, her liberal arts journalism degree yellowing with what she considered disuse, she'd been working as a news researcher–secretary–general "gofer" at a local television station in Columbia, Missouri, when Randell walked into her life. A popular, aggressive correspondent for a highly rated newsshow in Des Moines, Iowa, he'd come to Columbia for a guest lecture at the university's journalism school and had stopped by Nicole's station for an appearance on the lunchtime talk show—which was, she thought now, so prophetic. If only they'd known! She grinned and Rand misread the source of her pleasure.

"Talk about hogging the water! All you're doing is standing there grinning over having ousted me from my fair share. Move over, Missus."

She protested, but only halfheartedly. Her mind was still caught up in the past. They jockeyed for position, finally settling side-by-side beneath the spray. She stood quietly while he began soaping her shoulders and back and returned to her memories.

How upset, how furiously upset she'd been that day! After years of preparation, the closest she'd got to breaking into the business had been fetching coffee and checking facts for other reporters. It wasn't that she disliked gathering information or the almost constant telephone work—she was organized and highly efficient, and to a degree she enjoyed her job, but it wasn't what she wanted. Ambitious, impatient, aggressively certain she was meant for better things, Nicole had been chomping restlessly for the chance to do some *real* broadcast work. But when the opportunity finally came, she'd blown it.

An opening for street reporter at her station seemed like the answer to her dreams. It was what she'd been waiting for, working toward for so many years. Since about the time she'd shaved her eyebrows, in fact. . . . Her ninth-grade German class had written and staged a mock television program; Nicole had been selected as announcer. Despite her awkward performance in the harsh, guttural language, she'd been hooked. The feel of the microphone, the rustle of notes, the pressure of the tight schedule, had all thrilled her as few other things had ever done, before or since. She hadn't consciously decided just then to go into newscasting, but through high school she found herself participating in debate teams and speech contests, while excelling in the journalism classes. She'd been editor of her senior yearbook, the best yearbook Central High had ever seen, and by then, of course, she knew what it was she wanted to do with her life. With characteristic determination, she'd set out to get it.

It seemed her dream had finally arrived. But her air

check—the on-camera audition—had been miserable. It had been her own fault. Overanxious, overeager, she'd been nervously stiff, had spoken with exaggerated elocution in a voice much lower than her normal, comfortably modulated tones, and had shown as much animation as a lump of petrified wood. A superachiever, Nicole could never tolerate failure. She expected the best from herself and couldn't accept it when she produced anything less. She'd left the taping in a thunderous rage, furious with herself, ready to find something or someone on which to release all her pent-up disappointment and resentment. That someone had been Randell Clarke.

He stepped out of the studio where he'd taped his interview and smacked right into Nicole as she barreled blindly down the hall.

"Can't you look where you're going?" she snapped, not bothering to so much as glance at him.

"I can," he said, "but I obviously didn't. I'm sorry."

She looked up with a scowl that froze in place as she recognized his handsome features. Clarke's appearance had been the talk of the station's employees for days. He'd already made enough of a splash, though in a relatively small market, to be recognized as a rising media star. His well-groomed good looks coupled with his well-educated, intelligent expertise had people in the industry whispering that he was destined for the highly prized glory of network news. Females at the station had tended to concentrate rather more on his physical attributes and unmarried status, but Nicole had admired his achievements.

"It's okay," she muttered, still too angry to apologize as she knew she should. She took a step. He lightly clasped her arm and held her back. It was the excuse she'd wanted to really explode. "Would you mind?" she spat out. "I really don't have time to indulge you. I've work to do. The sort of work that stars like you take all the credit for."

He didn't appear to have heard. Or if he heard, he wasn't the sort to reach to insults. He simply stared down at her, taking in each feature of her face with such intensity that Nicole felt her anger slip away, replaced by something more potent. And far more disturbing.

"I didn't hurt you, did I?" he asked.

She shook her head mutely, suddenly unable to find her voice. "Good," he said, and smiled. Within the brilliant gleam of that smile, the last vestige of her ill humor vanished. It was the first of many such occasions, and now she rarely remembered she had a temper, much less ever lost it.

At the time, Rand had asked her to dinner and she'd astonished herself by accepting without a blink. Over a long, leisurely meal, a meal filled with laughter and conversation that seemed to escalate rather than decline as the evening wore on, she'd found herself telling him all about her audition and her frustration with her blown opportunity. He'd listened sympathetically until she muttered, "So much for dreams."

"Nobody hands you a dream," he calmly told her. "You have to work for it. The brighter the dream, the tougher the struggle to achieve it."

Looking directly into his understanding eyes, she'd felt a new, brighter-than-before dream sprout within her. By the end of the evening her anger and depression had been totally replaced by firm resolution. A few weeks later, she got a promotion—not on the air, but a step closer—and she sent Randell a bouquet of red roses with her thanks. He called her; it was the start of their long-distance relationship.

Their courtship was brief. Within six months, Nicole was searching for a job in Des Moines. When she was unable to find a job at any of the stations there, she stayed in Columbia, but they'd gotten married anyway, shocking family and friends who couldn't understand a marriage where the husband lived nearly three hundred miles away from his wife. They couldn't understand Nicole's determination to succeed in her career just as Randell was succeeding in his. They couldn't understand how a promotion to production assistant could mean more to her than a traditional marriage.

Only Rand had understood that she couldn't sacrifice her career on the altar of their love. He'd understood enough to put up with two years of married-but-apart life, two years of communicating through the static of the phone line, of enormous phone bills and exhausting weekend trips, two years of frustration as they tried to pack a week's worth of love, conversation, and companionship into forty-eight short hours. That is, forty-eight if they were lucky. Sometimes the weather or the news decided otherwise.

After one such weekend, when a late spring blizzard had ruined their plans to be together, Randell had sighed heavily into the phone. "We've been living like this long enough," he said. "I'm tired of being apart. I need you with me."

"Are you suggesting I leave my job here?" she countered, instantly defensive. It was almost reflexive, that response, an instinctive reaction after two years of veiling her hurt with pride and attempting to prove to parents, siblings, friends, that she and Rand were happy with their arrangement. They weren't. She hated it as much as he.

"I'm not about to just walk out on my job, Randell," she stated coldly.

"I'm not asking you to," he said. "I'm just saying we've got to look for something where we can be together. I love you. I need to be with you."

Hearing that soothing voice, she calmed and listened and agreed. She was willing to consider any scheme that would bring them—and their careers—together. But she'd never dreamed of just how together they'd soon be.

Both sent out applications and tapes to every market, large and small, throughout most of the Great Plains. For a few months, it was blackly discouraging. Interest in one rarely meant interest in the other, but they were determined to continue applying together and eventually, they hit pay dirt. Both were asked to audition for a station in St. Louis. They decided to do one air check together. The tape turned out well, extremely well. The relaxed, loving rapport between them came across the video screen, and the station's management instantly decided it liked the concept of a husband-and-wife team. They'd been hired within the week.

For Nicole it was a definite leap in her career. She'd at last be on the air, hosting a midday interview/news program for a sizable market. For Rand, it was something else again. It was, indeed, a move to a bigger market. But instead of reporting the sort of hard news he did best, he'd cohost the midday program, the type of show that was a fuzzy, sometimes uncomfortable combination of entertainment and news, the type of show any *real* newscaster scoffed at.

When Nicole hesitated about accepting the jobs, pointing out to Rand that he couldn't really consider a step down in career on her account, he had insisted their being together was more important than the position. "Besides," he pointed out, "it's only temporary. Something'll open up there. Or we'll head off to a bigger market. You know how this business is. A year or so at KSTL and we'll both be reporting hard news—there or somewhere else."

"A year or so" had stretched into four. Not that Nicole complained about it. They'd been four wonderful, very valuable years for her. She'd gained the on-camera experience she needed, experience that now made her one of the best television interviewers in the St. Louis market. She was relaxed, confident, and adept at extracting information from guests, whether they were garrulous or tongue-tied. She and Rand had channeled their drive toward a common goal, and together they'd turned *STL Noon* into the highest-rated program of its type in the market. They'd become highly popular and in demand as local celebrities.

Being with Randell constantly had also affected Nicole's personality. His calming influence had all but eliminated her once-famous fireworks flare-ups, which had in turn improved her ability on the job. Television, particularly television news, wasn't the place for artistic temperament. You had to work well with others, you couldn't permit yourself the luxury of getting upset easily—that was the lesson she'd learned from working with Randell.

One of the lessons, she amended as she sponged soap and water off his glistening chest. He had given her so much, professionally and privately, that the list of gifts would surpass the sum of the stars in a sapphire-bright night sky. The metaphor brought a tenderly loving lift to her lips, and seeing it, Rand bent quickly to kiss her.

"What's that for?" she asked when he pulled away.

"For having such a gorgeous smile," he answered, and

she knew another burst of happiness. *Could life get much better than this?* she wondered as he bent to kiss her again, more leisurely. The fine spray of water melted into their kiss, and Nicole decided, *No, it couldn't.* Life was perfect. Just perfect.

CHAPTER TWO

By the time they were ready to go on the air, they'd heard the rumor from six different sources. Ginny at the front desk had greeted them with it.

"You'll never guess what's in the wind this morning," she chirped with the smug aura of one who's about to impart Big News.

Exchanging an amused glance, Rand and Nicole paused expectantly. At every station there was one person whose primary function seemed to be cabling information from department to department. At KSTL if you wanted to know how much Lynn Johnson down in accounting paid for her root canal or when Barry Bosco stepped away from his camera long enough to move his bride into a three-bedroom house, you went to Virginia Heinemann. She ran the gossip wires as efficiently as she ran the switchboard, and with a great deal more relish.

As they waited Ginny cast a secretive glance around the empty brown-and-gold reception room, then leaned her plump form over the walnut grain of her desk and said in a conspiratorial whisper, "Craig McCall got here about an hour ago, and after being closeted with the Lion behind closed doors, the two of them went straight to Korsinski's office."

She returned to her cushioned chair with a soft plop. She riveted her eyes on Randell. He flicked his gaze from Ginny's softly rounded face to Nicole's delicately defined profile. Nicole studiously avoided meeting his eyes.

An unwonted and unpleasant chill oozed under her skin. Irrationally she wished they hadn't paused to hear Ginny's bit of gossip. She didn't understand the sudden erratic jump to her pulse and she felt rather foolish for it, so she simply stood waiting for Rand to make a move. After a long moment he returned his gaze to the receptionist and prompted, "From which we're to gather . . . ?"

"Well, I'm not saying it's a fact," she temporized, "but everyone knows that McCall's had his eye on the West Coast. Everyone knows he was in San Francisco in March. *If* he interviewed there and *if* he landed a job, there'd be a hole to fill in our evening news anchor team, now, wouldn't there?"

Her cheeks puffed out with satisfaction, saying more clearly than words could have done that she was certain there was no other possible explanation for Craig McCall's early-hour meetings with the station's news director and general manager. A light flashed brightly as the phone buzzed. Virginia reached for it, but let her hand hover over the receiver. "You'd be a perfect anchor for the station, Mr. Clarke," she said. "Simply perfect."

Neither Rand nor Nicole denied this. Neither said anything at all. As Ginny answered the call, they started down the wide corridor from which a tangle of large rooms sprouted like unrestrained leaves shooting haphazardly off a broad stem. The farther they progressed down the hall, the louder the clamor of men and machines emanated from those rooms to reverberate within their silent passage. Nicole's unaccustomed sense of unease seemed to increase with the volume. *A perfect anchor,* Ginny had said. But only to Rand . . .

A conflicting mixture of emotions wound through Nicole, twining and twisting together until none was clearly predominant. Indignation was there. Why single out Rand? *She'd* make a damn good anchor too! And a heady rush of adrenaline. It was time KSTL got with the competition and had a female anchor. She'd make a terrific anchor. Then she felt a slight contrition for the prick of pique, the intoxicating eagerness. How could she even consider dumping *STL Noon*? How could she consider leaving Rand on his own? And underscoring it all, confounding her most of all, was a panicky foreboding that set her heart to racing unsteadily.

Before they entered one of the quieter rooms, she chanced a look at her husband. His face told her nothing of his thoughts but bore his usual expression of sober thoughtfulness. With a deliberately casual air, she said, "If Ginny's latest tidbit turned out to be true, it would leave a hole, all right. About the size of the May ratings book."

Did she imagine that slight start, that almost guilty glance? Both flashed by for only the merest fraction of time; she couldn't be sure she'd truly seen them. Rand was smiling at her now, his usual crooked, charming smile.

"It's probably nothing more than grist for the gossip mill," he said. "You know how Ginny likes to build up any story she has to tell. Craig probably went to the Lion with a suggestion or a request and Ginny's blown it up into something sensational."

"It's awfully early for Craig to be here," she pointed out, watching him steadily.

He shrugged. "That could mean anything and nothing."

"But if it does turn out that he's leaving . . ."

"I'll leap into the corner farthest from Joe Korsinski's office," he said with a wide grin. "I wouldn't want to get trampled by the stampede of suppliants begging to be considered."

Her laugh was bright with understanding, but her gaze was dimmed by uncertainty. Would he leap out of the way . . . or would he head the stampede? Despite all the success of *STL Noon,* despite the accolades he'd won for his occasional feature series, Rand made no secret of his longing to return to hard news. Nicole knew he worried about the stigma of being considered an entertainer rather than a newsman; she also knew he couldn't be happy with the stagnation of his career over the past four years.

She strode into their office ahead of him, awash with self-reproach. It was she, after all, who'd been responsible for his leaving the prestigious excitement of hard news in the first place. Though at times she'd nearly forgotten it, the embers of her private guilt had never been completely doused. They'd worked so well together over the past four years, making their show the best it could be, raising ratings and wringing money and support from a reluctant news production staff. But none of that success had extinguished Nicole's nagging guilt. It flared now, threatening to reduce her earlier blithe mood to ashes. Needing reassurance, she turned her head to look at Rand and walked straight into Eva Baere.

Amid a flutter of papers the slender reporter steadied her, then laughed lightly, "You must still be reeling from the rumor that's bouncing around here."

Nicole smiled weakly and made vague noises of agreement. Rand cut in, asking Eva what she'd heard and from whom. Eyeing him speculatively from behind her lightly tinted glasses, Eva shoved a pencil into her golden puff of hair and told him the scuttlebutt was that McCall had tendered his resignation. She'd heard it from one of the engineers, who'd heard it from a production assistant for the night cast. Eva then scurried off, in a hurry to join the reporters flocking around the assignment editor in the main newsroom, leaving behind a tense pocket of silence.

"Do you believe it?" Nicole finally asked point-blank.

"Not any more than I believe any other unsubstantiated information," he answered.

There was no reason for his simple reply to disturb her, yet it did. He was being too noncommittal. The vague sensation of misgiving settled over her more heavily, a smothering shroud. It was senseless, this indefinable panic. She wasn't the sort to give reign to such unfounded emotions. She shook free of her lightweight linen jacket, determined to shake free of her unwarranted disquiet as well.

Paired to form two H-shaped units, four identical desks with built-in dividers and soft lighting created semiprivate cubicles within the open room. From the doorway it looked and sounded, at first, like any other office. A typewriter clacked, a telephone rang, papers shuffled over crowded desk tops. But any resemblance to a normal office ended with the videotapes. Videotapes lay everywhere. Jammed from floor to ceiling on Nicole's shelf, stacked in tottering towers on the floor beneath her desk, heaped in untidy clumps over the length and width of Rand's desk. At the far end of the room, centered between the last two cubicles, a color television was mounted over a video player. The set was always on; no one ever seemed to watch it.

As Rand turned to the first desk on the right, Nicole turned to the first one on the left. She carefully hung her beige jacket on a hook protruding from the side of a tall, narrow shelf behind her chair and meticulously smoothed her beige skirt before she sat. With four hours to go until airtime, she had to take care with her clothes, though since the time she'd spilled coffee down the front of a yellow shirtwaist ten minutes before going on the air, she always kept an extra outfit stashed in the car trunk for emergencies.

Randell scooped up a handful of the tapes currently decorating his desk. He'd spend the next hour or more viewing tapes from different sources, selecting what they'd use for today's program, then editing the tapes down to about a minute each. Because he'd had more news experience than she when they'd started doing *STL,* it had seemed natural that he do the major share of selecting and editing as well as writing the feature and news copy. Nicole had never resented it. She wrote the technical copy and handled most of the booking of guests. They worked well as a team. But as Randell headed toward one of the editing booths, Nicole had to repress the unusual urge to say "Let me do it this time."

Instead she dropped her woven purse into a bottom desk drawer and turned her attention to a scribbled sheet lying on her desk top. Last night's sports scores. Looking at it, she sighed audibly. It didn't matter to her anymore whether the Cardinals won or lost. Writing about it either way was incredibly boring. Just a routine. Maybe she was ready for a change after all. . . .

Shoving the perfidious thought aside, she rechecked the schedule for that day's show and mentally composed the teaser to be recorded later. The announcement would air at the top of the game show that preceded *STL Noon.* On Friday they had taped a series of station ID's with teasers that would run all this week, but they always recorded one the day of the show. She grabbed a sheet of blank paper, scored down the center with a thin line, rolled it into her typewriter, and struck the first keys.

Her concentration was complete whenever she immersed herself in the scripts. The only phone she ever heard ring was her own; the only voice she paid attention to was one directly addressing her. She no longer had to struggle to do this; years of experience enabled her to block out the clutter and babble surrounding her.

A shadow fell across the page, dimming her light. Frowning, she looked up. A professional display of perfect teeth dazzled her. The downturn of her mouth deepened. Although "pretty boy" newscasting had long since given way to poised journalism, Frank Walters could have made the grade in either category. He had the sort of square-jawed good looks that one normally found in soap opera stars. He also had the competent composure of a top-notch correspondent. Neither his ability nor his attractiveness, however, could equal the magnitude of his ego. Although everyone in the business had a certain amount of ego—they had to, or else they'd have elected for the relative anonymity of newspaper journalism—Nicole had never met anyone, anywhere, with one to match Frank's. She found it almost impossible to like someone with an ego the size of King Kong. On the other hand, Frank liked himself enough to make up for any lack of affection on her part.

She waited a second, then said coolly, "Need something, Frank?"

"No," he replied, teeth still flashing. He propped his lithe form on the corner of her desk and drawled conversationally, "I just wondered what you thought about this talk of McCall's resignation."

"I haven't thought about it. I've got too much work to do to waste time on rumors."

The clipped brevity of her reply didn't daunt him. You couldn't daunt a man like Frank. He had the sensitivity of a rhino. "Is it?" he asked.

"Is it what?"

"Is it just a rumor?"

Nicole longed to turn her shoulder on him and get on with her work, but he looked rather as if he intended to become a permanent paperweight on her desk top. He had the persistence that was the mark of every good newshound. She knew the only way to get rid of Frank was to give him the answers he wanted. With pointed emphasis, she flicked her typewriter to a dead silence and faced him fully.

"As far as I know it is. Why should you think I'd know any different? Craig's as closemouthed as they come."

"True, but if there's anyone he'd talk to, it'd be Rand."

"So why aren't you pestering Rand instead of me?"

He gave her the sort of look that sighed. She knew, of course, that even if Randell knew anything, he would keep it to himself. So would she, but Frank was sexist enough to think otherwise. After a perceptible pause, she said, "You probably know more than we do. The first we heard about this was when we arrived about fifteen minutes ago."

He scrutinized her for a few seconds, then shrugged and eased himself from her desk. "Okay. If I learn anything, I'll get back to you."

Sure you will, she mouthed to his retreating back, then swiveled forcefully around to her desk. As she punched her machine on, she fervently hoped she'd not hear another word about Craig McCall. Just fifteen minutes at work and she was already sick to death of the subject.

It was, of course, a vain hope. McCall seemed to be the exclusive topic of discussion that morning. Two things disturbed her even more than the unremitting prattle about McCall. Rand continued to avoid discussing it with her, and each time she heard the rumor from a new source, an unbidden, but undeniable excitement shook her more vehemently.

Almost of its own volition came an eager stream of thought. Joe Korsinski had a policy of promoting from within the station whenever possible. If a woman was considered . . . In all honesty, Nicole knew there was no other woman at the station as well qualified, as experienced, as suited to be an anchor as she. The street reporters like Eva might have an edge because they hadn't been tainted with the "soft" news prejudice, but she had something not one of them could possibly claim, and that was a viable audience.

She dammed the flow of such thoughts. It was a waste of time to indulge in reflection over gossip, and she didn't have time to waste. But her only respite from the deluge of gossip was while they were actually on air, and even then Nicole couldn't escape her obsession with it. During a commercial break she pretended to study the pink script sheets, but surreptitiously studied her husband instead. He was exchanging jokes with Barry and Ted, the cameramen, and looking as crisply fresh as if he'd just entered the studio. His blue vested suit somehow molded to his frame without creasing and his brown hair lay precisely in place. She no longer wondered how he managed to stay so well groomed—she'd watched too many times in awe as he merely shook his head to have his hair obediently look perfect—but she never stopped envying him for it. Her own dusky cut-to-the-shoulder crop seemed to be constantly on the verge of going out on strike, and the ruffles on her cinnamon chenille blouse had long since lost their starched edges. She couldn't deny that he looked like the perfect anchorman. . . .

With a wave of self-disgust at the pettiness of her thoughts, she cast the script sheets onto the round wicker table. Her hand narrowly missed knocking off a flat leaf of the hoya plant ornamenting the table's center. Without skipping a syllable in his conversation, Rand leaned forward and nudged the plant away from her. He cast her a private, special smile a heartbeat before he broadened it to include everyone in the studio.

Inwardly Nicole sighed. Ginny was right. Randell would make a perfect anchor. He had the poise, the ability to communicate in a relaxed but confident manner. Always before, his abilities had filled her with pride. At the moment they seemed to merely depress her. Looking at herself in the monitor, Nicole knew she would be just as capable. But would she be given the chance to prove it?

She caught herself up short on that. What was the matter with her, speculating and emoting over a damned ridiculous *rumor*? Why would she pay it any heed anyway? She was perfectly content with *STL*. She surveyed the small set, the "living room" of wicker table and chairs atop a patch of brown shag carpet, with Van Gogh's *Sunflowers* on the paneled wall and a bushy fern hanging by the window, and she told herself, yes, she was content here.

The floor director raised one arm with her palm extended above her head, signaling that the camera was about to be switched on. "Stand by for two," she said.

Nicole straightened almost imperceptibly in her wicker chair, smoothing her linen skirt as she did so. Sharla brought her hand down to point at camera two, and facing it, Nicole said, "Welcome back to *STL Noon.* We're especially glad to have you with us because we've got a special treat for you today."

"That's right," put in Rand, smiling into the lens of camera one and reading off the TelePrompTer. "After receiving a ton of requests from all of you for the past month, we're ready to cry uncle. We're giving in and bringing back our 'On the Town' feature, starting with this look at only the fourth garden of its kind in the world, the Laumeier Sculpture Garden."

With the wizardry of modern technology the home viewers saw a pretaped cassette that had already had the voice tracks cut, so Rand and Nicole were able to lean back and relax once more. "We're right on time," Sharla told them with a cheery smile that her headset couldn't hide. They nodded in response. Rand pulled a can of cola from beneath the table and sipped; Nicole looked at the monitor to her left, the one showing what the home audience saw. Watching Rand tour the garden on the screen, she was pricked by another of those disquieting sensations of foreboding. Without fully understanding why, she wished the rumor were nothing more than that, an empty rumor.

It could be true. It probably was. Most people in the business were restless, anxious to move on, willing to hopscotch from one market to another as they aimed for the brass ring of network news. Craig McCall was as ambitious as most.

The phone at her elbow rang, startling Nicole. She glanced to the cubicle across the way. Rand took a bite out of the roast beef sandwich he held in his left hand while scribbling notes on a legal pad with his right. Since Monday they hadn't really talked about McCall's possible departure. Their one discussion about it had been oddly guarded, neither of them willing to come out and ask what she knew they both wanted to ask: *Are you going to apply for it?*

For the rest of the week, the subject had been scrupulously avoided. It was a disturbing first, this not discussing a touchy subject. Always before, she and Rand had communicated with a rare openness; they'd always been able to share doubts and fears as well as joys and triumphs. They'd even set a rule about it: Never go to bed with a misunderstanding between them. But this wasn't a misunderstanding. It wasn't anything. They hadn't fought over it. They hadn't even talked about it. Monday had somehow melted into Friday without McCall's name again cropping up in their conversations.

But it lay between them, an invisible chalked line neither dared to cross. . . .

The second loud summons from the phone made her jump. She yanked the receiver up and said, "Yes?" rather sharply.

"If you want to talk about that sewing segment, get in here" was the huffy statement preceding the abrupt click.

Knowing full well that Lionel Pinder meant what he said, Nicole immediately hung up and stood with a determined little swish to her flared skirt. Rand looked up, then grinned with sympathetic understanding. She grimaced and made comic-book motions of rolling up her sleeves, even though the puffed sleeves on her navy-and-red abstract print dress were already cuffed at the elbow. He gave her a thumbs-up sign as she marched out.

She was glad for the encouragement. Jousting with the news director over the orientation of their program was one of the least enjoyable aspects of their job, and like most other things, they shared the disagreeable task. It was her turn to present their latest argument. She raised her chin and sailed into the main newsroom, armor-plated and ready for battle.

The newsroom was noisy, crowded, and palpably tense. Cubicles exactly like those in her own office formed several aisles, but here they hummed with incessant activity while lights more glaring than soft illuminated the scene. In the farthest corner a group of desks formed a room within the room, the office for the producers. Nicole went directly to a cubicle at the edge of the cluster.

Lionel sat hunched over his desk, wearing a crinkled pale pink shirt and a perpetually harried look as he stabbed a blunt pencil at a dull yellow sheet of news copy. Wiry wisps of ashen hair shot out from his balding skull. Lines trenched across the width of his shining brow. A cigarette tilted precariously from his clamped lips and coils of smoke furled around his head, looking like small tornadoes bent on destruction whenever he moved. Without looking up he gestured impatiently for Nicole to take the vacant chair at his side.

She'd rather have stood, but she took the indicated seat and waited. He ignored her for several long minutes, then abruptly shoved aside a schedule sheet and swiveled to face her. "You look like a Jackson Pollock painting in that damned dress," he said by way of greeting.

"Thank you," she responded calmly. She knew the remark for the offensive tactic it was. He meant to set her at a disadvantage from the first, but Nicole wasn't about to be deterred from getting what she and Rand wanted. She took a deep breath and got directly to the point. "The sewing segment has to be dropped, Lionel."

He puffed silently on his cigarette, studying her through the gray clouds of smoke. Finally he stubbed the cigarette into a green ashtray already overflowing with ashes and butts. He leaned back in his chair. "That segment's been a part—a very popular part—of *STL Noon* since the show first went on the air."

"Which is one reason it should go. It's been around too long; it's exhausted its possibilities as an interesting feature. Beyond which, Rand and I think *STL* should focus more on news features. We think that's what you'd want as well."

"What I want or you want doesn't mean a damn," Lionel grunted. He spoke with one side of his mouth lifted and the other pressed tightly together, as if still holding his ever present cigarette between his thin lips. "What matters is that the powers-that-be focus on ratings. They like the ratings they see for *STL* and they don't want to rock the boat."

"But ratings can be improved. *STL* can be improved.

The final decision is yours, Lionel. Why are you so resistant to this suggestion?"

He tapped a battered pack of cigarettes on his cluttered desk top, drew one out, and lit it. Sighing heavily, he blew out a gust of smoke. "If you want to drop the sewing, drop it, *but—*"

She narrowed her gaze at him. "But . . . ?"

"But don't replace it with anything that's going to take any more crew or money. I can't spare you either one."

His chair squeaked in loud protest as he whirled back to his desk. The interview was over.

Nicole started to rise, then paused. Impulsively she leaned forward and said on a rush, "Lionel, you must know by now there's a rumor afloat that McCall's leaving. Is it true?"

His gaze slewed her way through a whirlwind of gray smoke that clung to the wisps of his hair. "What's it matter to you?"

She met his assessing gaze directly. "I could be interested in applying for the vacancy."

He narrowed his eyes, lowering his shaggy brows in an intimidating stare, before he turned his back to her. The rumples in the pink shirt shifted as he shrugged. "A rumor is a rumor."

She waited. Phones shrieked. Unintelligible voices babbled. Lionel studiously shuffled through a sheaf of papers. Realizing what she'd already expected—that the Lion wouldn't divulge a thing—Nicole rose and returned to her office.

Rand wasn't at his desk, which relieved her. She didn't want to face him until she'd faced the facts. Lionel's brusque "What's it matter to you?" had jolted her into realizing that she wanted, she very much wanted, to apply for that anchor position. *If* that anchor position were going to be available. But she didn't want to face Rand with her revelation. She knew without asking that he'd want to apply, too, and she had to think it out before she spoke with him about it.

Of course, he'd want her to apply. He'd always been very supportive of her career. Though they'd never before been competitors for a position, she was still certain he'd tell her to go ahead. So why was she feeling reluctant?

Because that ominous chill had seeped into her blood again. And again she had to wish that the damned rumor would prove to be nothing else.

She set to work editing the tape for Monday's "Hometown Views" feature. In addition to her duties for *STL Noon,* she did two features a week for the evening news, one a collection of views from the public on a current topic, such as this week's "Do you think enough is being done to refurbish the riverfront?" The other feature was a highlight of a local nightspot or restaurant, "Gateway Nightlife." She usually went out with a crew on Tuesdays and Thursdays for taping, then edited the film the next day for airing on Mondays and Wednesdays. She finished cutting the voice track and returned to her desk, feeling immeasurably better. In the solitude of the small editing booth she'd expunged her irrational fears. She had no reason to dread McCall's leaving and every reason to hope it was true. After all, such career opportunities didn't come along very often.

So when Rand strolled in and asked her how many fingers the Lion had bitten off, she grinned and said merrily, "All of them, and my toes to boot. But we got the segment dropped."

He plopped into his chair and loosened his tie. "I knew

no mere news director would be a match for you," he said with satisfaction.

She perched on the corner of his desk and shook her head. "Oh, he more than matched me. He informed me in no uncertain terms that whatever we use to fill the hole, we can't have any extra crew or money."

"Now, why doesn't that surprise me?" He stretched out a finger and ran it lightly over the curve of her calf. "So what else did he have to snarl at you about?"

She could feel her skin rising in the path of his fingertip. The sheer hose seemed to melt beneath his touch. It was an effort to collect her thoughts enough to answer him. "Um, the rumor about McCall."

Rand's finger paused. She looked down at his hand, poised a breath from her leg, then up at him. He met her look with one of inquiry—and something else, something dark and predatory. She wished she hadn't said anything. She looked away and attempted a shrug. "I asked him if it was true. Naturally he did little more than growl at me." She hunched her shoulders and deepened her voice to a low pitch. " 'A rumor is a rumor.' "

"You must know, Coley," he said, softening the harshness of his tone with his special pet name for her, "that if it's not, if McCall's really leaving, I'm going to apply for the position."

"I'd expect you to," she responded instantly. "It's what you've always wanted."

His hand circled her calf, slid upward. He tickled the back of her knee. "What about you?" he asked. "Would you put in an application?"

"Of course I would."

"Such hesitation. Are you sure?"

"Are you?"

He chuckled and skated his hand up over her thigh. The silky folds of her skirt stirred in soft rustles as his fingers swirled. She inched her leg toward the edge of his desk, but his hand went with her.

"Randell," she admonished.

"Nicole," he mimicked. Then he smiled and she forgot her objections. She relaxed and let his fingers roam at will. It was, after all, nearly time to go home.

"I wouldn't want you not to try for it," he said abruptly. "You've always stretched yourself to achieve the best, and I wouldn't want you to stop doing that, for any reason."

The fingers teasing her thigh were highly distracting, but she managed to carry on her end of the conversation. "Maybe," she said a shade breathlessly, "it's a good thing it's just a rumor."

"Maybe," he agreed, and something in the toneless word resurrected all her apprehensive presentiments. And again she was torn between hoping the rumor were true and wishing it weren't.

CHAPTER THREE

The announcement came within the hour, just before the first evening broadcast at five. As of the end of July, Craig McCall would be leaving to work at a prestigious station in San Francisco. Lionel finished the terse statement with a pronouncement that a replacement had not yet been decided upon.

Nicole thought it distinctly odd that her pulse could accelerate and her heart plummet at one and the same instant.

"Just our luck," whispered Rand into her ear. "The first rumor in the history of KSTL to be proved totally accurate and it has to be this one."

She glanced up at his irreverent grin. "You only look so smug because you're the logical choice to replace him," she whispered back.

"Unless management decides it's time to hire a woman to co-anchor with Gene Thompson."

Lionel discharged heavy puffs of smoke as he exhorted

everyone to get on with work. The low buzz of reaction momentarily swelled, each person there having an opinion to voice. Rand tipped his head toward the door; Nicole nodded in agreement. They threaded through the clamorous throng of bodies crowding the newsroom and down a bare passageway. Though leggy—her brothers had always called her "Colt" during adolescence—Nicole had trouble keeping up with Rand's long, easy strides. Once they were well beyond the exit, however, he slowed and let her catch up to his side.

"You know what I think?" he asked, flashing a smile at her.

"No, what do you think?" she returned.

"I think we deserve a treat. It's been a hellish week and I, for one, don't want to face burger casserole direct from our microwave."

"You'd prefer eating from someone else's microwave, is that it?"

"That's it. I'm famished and feel like being waited on." As he spoke, he took hold of her arm and steered her through the parking lot. When he reached their compact sedan, he paused. "Any objections?"

"Not in the least. Actually, if you hadn't suggested it, I would have." She slid into the gray upholstered seat and tossed a tired smile at him. "As you say, it's been a hellish week."

They left the lot in silence, letting the tension of the week dissipate in the heated sunlight coating the interior. A strip of light struck the white gold of Nicole's wedding band, capering over its smooth surface and catching her eye. She stared at the gleaming width, then rubbed her thumb across it. The solid weight of her ring had always felt so special to her, signifying the substance of her marriage. Now she felt the burden of it and wondered resentfully why her marriage and career should conflict so much more often than other people's. She loved Rand, but she loved her work too. Why should the two be so incompatible? It wasn't fair.

The reality was, of course, that the two hadn't been so incompatible at all. In fact, over the past four years they'd gone hand-in-glove. Her relationship with Rand had meant sharing career as well as marriage goals. But now, for the first time, it appeared they were going to be competitors rather than collaborators. Surely their relationship was strong enough to handle it.

Her indistinct fears were crystallizing. Rand was every bit as aggressively ambitious as she herself was. Inevitably, competing for the same job would affect their personal relationship. Would they be able to withstand the pressures? She pressed her ring into her finger, digging the metal into the skin, and vowed that they would.

"I hope you're hungry," said Rand, and Nicole was jolted into awareness as the car slowed.

Rand parked in front of an unprepossessing white frame building with chipped red lettering scripted over a plate glass window that read MAMA'S. Nicole smiled with heartfelt pleasure. He glanced at her. "I said we deserved a treat."

"This is perfect," she said, and he visibly preened.

The building's faintly disreputable exterior was deceptive. Although the interior design was limited to candles stuck in old wine bottles and a few baskets hanging on the walls, a vibrant warmth and cheer permeated the open room. Aromatic steam filled the air, the clash and clatter of pans resounded from the kitchen, and a continually boisterous chatter passed among the customers and

Mama's help. Several fine restaurants attracted heavy crowds to the Hill, St. Louis's Italian neighborhood, but Mama's wasn't one of them. Mama's was the Hill's gathering place, where neighbors met to catch up on gossip, to flirt outrageously, and to enjoy some of the best pasta this side of Rome.

Rand and Nicole had discovered it by accident. A tragic hotel fire several months previous had kept them at the station late into the night, working without thought for the meal they'd missed or the long hours they'd put in that day. The emotional backlash was inevitable. As they drove home, weary and worn out, they'd snipped at one another pettishly, arguing over where to look for a meal, until Rand had braked sharply and stated "There's a place. We'll eat there."

"There?" Nicole had asked doubtfully, wrinkling her nose at Mama's peeling paint and dilapidated appearance. She'd subsided into silence at the exasperated glare he'd thrown at her. They had been pleasantly surprised by the clean, cheery interior and even more surprised by the superb food. Though they'd often talked about returning, they'd never yet got around to it; even so, they were greeted at the door like family.

With an energetic wave of a spindly arm, a small man scampered toward them. He wiped his hands on a sauce-spattered apron knotted around his waist and grasped Rand's hand. Pumping it vigorously, he smiled radiantly. "I've been holding your table for you," he said.

"But we—" began Nicole, only to be stopped by another expansive wave of his hand.

"You don't think we forgot our celebrities?" The shocked tone was emphasized by a click of his teeth. Before either could say anything, he spun around and yelled, "Hey, Louie, a bottle of the Recioto!" He turned back to them and added, "On the house," then bustled the pair toward a table pressed against the far paneled wall.

Numerous eyes, some curious, some puzzled, some slightly embarrassed, followed their progress. For the most part Nicole and Rand didn't notice the fixed stares and hurried glances. Over the past few years they'd become accustomed to them. Nicole occasionally wished she weren't so often on display, but having to maintain a public image was part of the price for doing what she wanted to do.

As she sat she smiled and said graciously, "It's very kind of you to remember us. But tell Mama the wine is unnecessary. We couldn't—"

"Nonsense! Of course you can. I insist." The apron fluttered and the sleeveless T-shirt puffed out as the waiter reached for his full height. "*I* am Mama," he said proudly.

Rand quelled Nicole's impulse to giggle with a warning glance before presenting his most charming smile to the proprietor. "We're pleased to be able to meet you, to be able to tell you in person how much we're looking forward to another of your unbelievably delicious meals. We've talked of it for months."

"Mama" left them with two worn, grease-spotted menus and a beaming grin. After a few minutes and without looking at her, Rand said in a barely even voice, "Thank you, Mrs. Clarke."

"You're welcome, Mr. Clarke," she replied on an equally unsteady note.

"That laugh of yours was smothered in a good cause," he went on, still intently studying his menu.

"I'll do what I can to preserve the dignity of the *STL*

hosts," she said gravely, then ruined the noble effect by giving in to a small giggle.

He lowered his menu. His dark eyes reflected tiny pinpoints of candlelight. Within them, Nicole saw a wealth of love, and she was captivated by the glow of it. He set his fingertips to his lips and blew her a kiss. She raised her hand, intending to return the kiss, but a hesitant voice halted the gesture.

"Are you the ones, you know, the ones that do that show on TV?"

She caught Rand's brief smile of amused resignation before she turned to the woman standing beside their table. "Yes," she replied with a nod, "we're the ones. We host *STL Noon.*"

The woman's full face altered, shifting from cautious inquiry to shining satisfaction. Her black curls bounced in all directions as she bobbed her head vigorously. "I thought so. I thought you were the ones. Didn't I tell you they were the ones?" she demanded of a trio sitting at a table nearby.

"I hope you like the program," said Nicole, and immediately castigated herself mentally. She must be more tired than she'd thought. She knew better than to make such a remark. It invited conversation. Her hope that the invitation wouldn't be accepted was quickly dashed. Setting her hands on her ample hips, the woman pursed her mouth as she considered the question.

"Well, I don't watch it much," she admitted finally, "but I like it okay. But I gotta tell you that show you had with that fancy young woman who said how more day-care centers were needed, well, that show was a big mistake. That woman just didn't know what she was talking about."

Nicole knew she should smile politely and firmly raise her menu, but the woman's forceful indignation intrigued her. "What do you mean?"

"You tell me, who's gonna raise your kids better than you? It takes a mother to teach a kid what's what, not some day-care center. You oughta have a mother on to talk about raising kids."

"Perhaps we should. I'll mention it to our news director."

Her flabby arms jiggled as she wagged a finger at Nicole. "That's right. You do that." More curls jounced in a nod of parting as the woman left them alone. They heard her saying, "What did I tell you?" as she ambled back to her seat. "Did I tell you they were the ones?"

By dint of focusing on the candle stub perched lopsidedly in an old green wine bottle, by steadfastedly refusing to so much as glance at her husband, Nicole managed to smother her second upswelling of mirth.

But in the interlude before Mama reappeared with their wine, her good humor faded. They discussed today's program, next week's schedule, their plans for the weekend. As they had all week, they skirted the one crucial issue. It seemed to Nicole to be a palpable barrier between them. The feeling was new and unpleasant. She and Rand didn't have barriers like that between them. Or at least they hadn't up to now. Without knowing quite how to go about it, Nicole resolved to knock it down before it became insurmountable. As soon as Mama took their orders and again departed, she confronted it head-on.

"Rand, I—we're—" She paused, took a breath, and tried again. "This is ridiculous. We're avoiding the one thing I know we're both thinking about. We can't go on tiptoeing around the subject as if it didn't exist. Our marriage has always been based on open communication. So let's communicate."

"That sounded like a good bit of communicating to me," teased Rand.

A frown hardened the line of her mouth. She didn't want to joke about this. She wanted to *talk*. "Rand, I'm serious," she said in a low voice that told him just how serious she was.

He picked at a bit of multicolored wax coating the bulbous bottle supporting the candle. "I know, honey. But I'm not sure what it is you want me to say. I want McCall's position. I know you want it. I know one of us isn't going to get it. What else is there to say?"

Flickers from the candle shadowed the structure of his face, softening it. Nicole watched his grim expression fade within the wavering light and felt love and hurt rush through her, pushing against each other. She didn't know what she wanted him to say, but that hadn't been it. She didn't want to hear bald facts, she wanted to hear that everything was going to be all right, that nothing was going to mar their marriage. She wanted reassurance. She hadn't gotten it.

"I don't know," she said, feeling helplessly unsure. "But it's not healthy for us not to talk about it. That doesn't make the problem go away."

He looked up, narrowing his gaze. "Is there a problem?"

"I don't know that either."

After what seemed an interminable hesitation, Rand reached over and cupped his hand over Nicole's. His wedding band glinted. "There's no problem. Not if we don't make it into one. So long as we love each other, the job shouldn't make any difference to us."

Relief, sweet and pure, swept away her mounting fears. He sounded so unalterably certain. He made her feel certain too. It was precisely the reassurance she'd needed. "I do love you," she whispered.

His grip on her hand tightened briefly, then he released her and straightened in his chair. "It'll all be over in a couple of months anyway. With McCall leaving at the end of July, a decision about a replacement would be made by the end of June, mid-July at the latest."

"Do you think we'll have to do an audition? It would be pretty absurd, don't you think? Joe should have some idea of what we're each capable of by now."

Rand mulled for several seconds before responding in a slow drawl. "Absurd, but very like our esteemed general manager. I'd be willing to lay money he'll make us do an air check. He'll say it's to keep the other applicants from crying foul. I suppose in a way he'll be right."

Nicole swirled a fingertip over the tablecloth, tracing the outline of a cigarette burn in the checkered plastic. She fixed her gaze on the shine of her clear nail polish as her finger looped up, then down, then up again. "I'm certain Frank Walters is going to apply. He's been practically salivating since the first day the rumor got out. Anyone else from the station you think will give it a shot?"

"I don't know. It's hard to tell what evil ambition lurks in the hearts of fellow workers."

"If he does apply, Frank will be considered seriously." She intently retraced the dark brown pattern. "So will you."

"And you."

She raised her eyes. His were filled with tender pride. Her pulse rushed with joy to have him look at her like that. How lucky she was to have Randell's love—and his respect. What she didn't have was his reporting experience.

"I don't—" she started.

"You've got the qualifications for the position, Nicole, and a definite edge over Walters in personality and looks."

Loyalty too. She had Rand's loyalty. His loyalty, his respect, his love. Nothing else really seemed to matter. Her joy spilled over into a lighthearted laugh. "Don't lay it on too thick, darling," she admonished. "*Nobody* has an edge over Frank Walters in looks."

He chuckled and agreed. "Still, given Joe's policy of promoting from within and the other possible in-house competition, I can't help but feel that the new KSTL anchor is sitting right here."

"And does your masculine intuition tell you which one of us it is?" she asked, just a shade tartly.

In answer Rand shrugged and lifted his wineglass. The deep red liquid sloshed slightly against the sides. "May the best man—"

"Or woman," she cut in.

"Or woman," he acknowledged with a broad smile. "May the best *person* win."

Their glasses met with a solemn *clink*. Equally solemnly they sipped the wine. The small ceremony seemed imbued with a significance far outweighing the simple toast.

"Actually," said Rand as he lowered his glass, "that's an empty sort of toast. It implies that one of us must be better than the other, when really we're both well qualified for that anchor spot."

"Umm," agreed Nicole. "The sad fact is that qualifications probably won't count for much. It'll probably come down to something as ridiculous as whether or not they want a woman."

"Or whether they want someone who's fresh on the scene."

"Or whose face best complements Gene Thompson's."

"Or which set of teeth is capped best."

"Oh, not teeth," she moaned. "Anything but teeth. If it comes down to teeth, Frank's got it, no contest."

Suddenly both were laughing. The laughter cleansed the air, wiped away that hint of constraint that had been threatening to divide them. Rand took her hand in his and held it like a new lover anxious for each opportunity to touch his beloved. He stroked the inside of her palm with his thumb. The slow, sensuous caress made Nicole feel wanted—and slightly wicked. She was tempted to suggest skipping the meal and going straight home.

By the time they did head for home, sent off with a flourish and a second bottle of wine from Mama, Nicole was feeling utterly content. Her veal scaloppine had been delicious; she felt sated. The red wine, though drier than she usually liked, had had a full flavor that enhanced her appreciation of the meal and of the man with her. Their conversation had been punctuated by small silences, but silences more companionable than strained. They'd left arm-in-arm, drowsily satisfied with life in general and each other in particular.

The sky had a dark purplish hue, like a wild plum with dewy drops of stars sparkling over its surface. Nicole contemplated the beauty of it through half-closed eyes.

"What are you thinking?"

She turned her head at Rand's soft query. His profile was sharply cast, each feature so finely molded, it took her breath away. She loved that profile. She loved that man. Sometimes, like now, her love seemed so enormous, so overwhelming, it made her heart hurt in her chest to think of it.

He glanced toward her. "You alive? Or playing 'possum?"

The hurt melted away, leaving only pure, sweet love. She smiled and laughed breathily. "You'd better watch the road."

"I'd much rather watch you," he said, but he obediently returned his gaze to the road. "So what were you thinking?"

"I was thinking how beautiful the sky is tonight. But I've decided it's nothing compared to you. You're the most beautiful thing in my life."

"Now, how," he asked on a note of exasperation, "do you expect me to keep my mind on my driving when you talk to me like that?"

She stretched out her hand and slowly caressed his thigh. "Oh, you'll manage. You always do."

His laugh was nearly a groan. Her hand crept upward. The car sped forward.

They did not bother to switch on the lights. They did not pull the drapes. The wine bottle was discarded haphazardly on the Indian-print cushions of the sofa. Like Hansel and Gretel's bread crumbs, colorful bits of clothing marked a trail from the front door to the bedroom.

Lambent moonlight shimmered over them, gilding their bodies with a vibrant glow. The luminous brilliancy thrilled Nicole. It enabled her to study the lean lines of Rand's body, to watch the shifting of muscle and sinew, to see the excitement she raised in him. The way he responded to her had always added to the pleasure she took from him. Knowing she could rouse him so thoroughly made her feel special. She always felt special with Rand.

He lay on his back, bathed in moonbeams. She bent over him, mantling his body with her shadow. She splayed her fingers over his chest, trapping the smooth skin beneath her touch. The thump of his heart beat against her palm. The thump of her own accelerated.

Reaching up, Rand cupped her breasts within his hands. She closed her eyes. Gently, lightly, his palms circled, grazing her stiffened nipples, brushing the soft undersides. She drew in a long breath. His mouth nuzzled first one taut nipple, then the other. She exhaled that breath and opened her eyes. Layers of creamy light caught the flaxen in his brown hair and wove it into pure gold. It reminded Nicole of an ancient golden idol, to be cherished above all else. She did cherish him. She adored him. She pressed a worshipful kiss into the silken midst of his hair.

He raised his head. They stared at each other without speaking. She felt her love and desire expand until it outshone the moon. Slowly, enraptured within the radiant light, she lowered her mouth to the magic of his.

Their love melded together in a binding kiss. Nicole gripped his shoulders and his heated flesh seared her fingertips. As the passion of their kiss deepened, she inched her fingers toward his neck and with tantalizing brevity, caressed the sensitive spot behind his ears. The result was as she'd known it would be. His breathing quickened and his pulse raced out of control. She blew a light, triumphant laugh into their kiss.

He ran his hands restlessly down the ridge of her spine. "You . . . are . . . a tease," he whispered hoarsely.

She dropped a tiny kiss on his chin and slipped out of

his reach. She stretched her arms upward, knowing his gaze avidly followed the motion. "But you love it," she said on a husky note of certainty.

"I love *you,*" he corrected.

"And you love it when I tease." She came upright on her knees. Black waves billowed as she tossed her head back. She heard his breath stagger and felt giddy with pleasure. To affect Rand this way intoxicated her more than any wine, however heady, possibly could.

Rand propped himself up on an elbow. He said nothing, but his tense immobility proclaimed his need for her. Nicole felt his passion. She felt it in the clenching of her stomach, the rushing of her blood, the tightening of her muscles. Desire crackled in the small space between them. When he drawled, "Come here," she forgot about teasing him, forgot about everything except her need to be in his arms.

Gliding into his embrace, she kissed him with a fierce passion that he fully returned. He grasped her hips and, still locked within that consuming kiss, lifted her onto him. His hands skimmed over her skin, raising tingles and temperature from her soft breasts to her curving hips to the moist center of her being. His touch was elusive, electrifying. Sweat began to slick their bodies, yet Nicole shivered.

Goosebumps rose over her skin, springing up wildly wherever his fingers danced, his lips darted. He traced the contour of her breasts with his tongue. He teased the curve of her buttocks with his hands. He chased away her goosebumps with heated strokes, rousing her to a feverish pitch. There was not an inch of her flesh he didn't know how to inflame, and he used his knowledge completely.

When she shoved aside his hands and opened herself to

him, she heard the heavy catch of his breath, but only faintly. Sensations far stronger than sound enveloped her. She was beyond everything but the shattering pleasure of having him within her. Her body was taut with concentration as Rand thrust up to meet her.

The beauty of the night encased them in a wondrous enchantment. Each caress captivated, each kiss enthralled, each driving delight brought them toward a deeper source of fulfillment. They strained together and together reached new heights of ecstasy.

Tumbling over the peak, Nicole collapsed atop him. The carousel of her senses gradually stopped spinning. She nuzzled her cheek against his chest. The clamor of his heartbeat drummed loudly in her ear. She licked him, tasting the salty sweat coating him.

He feathered his hands through the riot of her hair. "Do that again," he said.

"Do what? This?" she asked, flicking her tongue over his chest. She heard his sharp intake. With an impish laugh, she wiggled her hips over his midriff. "Or did you mean this?"

"I said you were a tease," he told her, half laughing, half gasping. With a swift motion he rolled her over onto her back and bent over her. "And do you know what happens to women who tease?"

She saw his intent too late. Her attempt to slide out from his clasp never had a chance of success. He gripped her by the sides and began tickling from underarm to rib, over her stomach and back again. She flailed her arms, kicked her legs, and shrieked, "Rand! Stop! Please stop!"

It amazed her how fingers that could evoke such delight a moment before could now torture her so. She hated to be tickled and he knew it. Though she laughed, it was without humor. Finally she gritted her teeth and sputtered, "If you don't stop now . . . I'm going to get mad."

He laughed, but pulled away. "Now you know what happens to a tease."

"You should talk," she muttered, but she wasn't really angry and she knew he knew it.

He stretched out on his back beside her. He caught hold of her hand and twined his fingers with hers. They lay quietly, watching strips of moonlight skim about the room.

"You're right," said Rand after a time. "Tonight was beautiful."

"I was right about you too," she said. "You're beautiful."

A breeze waltzed through the window. The unexpected chill of it brought a quiver to Nicole. He leaned down and pulled the sheet up over her. "But nothing compares with you," he said, almost reluctantly. "I love you, Coley. Don't ever forget that."

He sounded so serious. And oddly hesitant. Another shudder coursed through her. He tucked the sheet more closely about her. She licked her lips. "I— Thank you," she said.

"Can't have you catching cold," he returned.

She knew he'd understood she was thanking him for more than the sheet, but she let it pass. "I'm glad we went back to Mama's, aren't you?"

"Umm. I'm especially glad for the wine." His hand wandered over her thigh. She slapped it away. "Shall we open the other bottle?" he asked suggestively.

"You, Randell Clarke, have a one-track mind."

"But you'll at least admit, darling, that it's on the right track."

She vehemently disclaimed admitting any such thing. He immediately set out to convince her. She didn't take much convincing. When he drew back from a long, deeply persuasive kiss, she sighed happily. "I've been thinking," she said.

"Nicole, my love, let me explain to you that now is not the time for thinking."

"I've been thinking," she went on, unperturbed, "about the impact we have."

"You have a big impact on me," he agreed and nibbled the lobe of her ear.

"That woman tonight, the one who was so indignant about day-care centers. She said she doesn't watch our show that much, yet she was up in arms over that issue." Nicole restlessly flapped her hands over the sheet, a gesture that always indicated a level of intensity within her. "We affect people, Rand. That's a lot of power. It makes me wonder about the power of being an anchor, having that kind of steady audience."

"So don't apply," he said flippantly.

A spurt of anger shot through her. She whipped her head toward him and snapped, "Don't brush this off. We have to talk about it. Didn't we agree about that?"

"Of course we did. I'm sorry, Coley, I was just trying to be funny. I guess it fell flat."

"Like a rock."

He raised up and looked down at her. His face was too shadowed for her to read, but she heard the love in his voice. "I know. I didn't mean to brush it off, honestly. But I told you before, I'm not sure what it is you want me to say. Surely you already know that the power of the position is one of the reasons I want the job. I'm sure it's one of the reasons you want it too."

"I suppose so," she confessed reluctantly. "But I don't think I've considered before just how far-reaching that power is."

"All the better for us to keep Frank Walters from exercising his sway over the unsuspecting public," Rand drawled.

This time she curled her hand into a sturdy fist and beat on his back. "Don't make jokes, dammit! Talk to me!"

"I'll talk, I'll talk. I'll tell you anything you want to know. Just please don't beat me anymore, please!"

She fell back into her satin pillow with an annoyed laugh. "Why is it that I can't stay mad at you? It ought to be one of the rules of fair fighting that you're not allowed to make your opponent laugh in the middle of the fight."

He rolled over, holding himself a breath above her. "I love to hear you laugh, Coley. I love you, period. It's because I love you, I don't like to argue with you, about anything. If it's talk you want, I'm willing to talk, but not to argue."

She toyed with the silky ends of his hair, then let her hands drift down his nape. "We weren't arguing. But something certainly wasn't right between us. What happened, Rand? Why didn't we talk?"

"Perhaps because we both feared hurting the other one, even a little. Perhaps because we feared being hurt. I don't know. I know I'm glad we went out tonight. And I'm damn glad you're so persistent. If anything will keep the air clear between us, it'll be your persistence."

His breath nuzzled her cheek. She felt the warmth of it caress her and knew an urge to wrap herself within it. She wound her arms about him, squeezing so tightly that he choked on a small bit of laughter.

"Whatever happens," she said fiercely, "don't let it divide us, Rand. Don't let anything ever come between us."

"If you . . . continue to hold me . . . in this hammerlock," he gasped, "nothing possibly could."

CHAPTER FOUR

"I just don't understand you, Nicole. Not at all. A wife should support her husband, not surpass him. Why do you have to compete with Rand?" The exasperation in Dee's question hummed across the phone line and was followed instantly by a long-suffering sigh. "I suppose you don't see anything wrong with a wife wanting to outdo her husband."

"I'm not trying to outdo Rand," said Nicole with carefully controlled patience. She told herself it was only natural that Rand's older sister wouldn't understand. She might have believed it, too, if her own family weren't just as vocally opposed to her applying for the anchor position.

"I don't know what else you'd call it when you try to take a job away from him."

"I'm not taking anything away from him. There's no guarantee either one of us will get that job—"

"But why do you even have to try for it?" Dee broke

in. She sounded almost as peevish as Nicole felt. "A wife should—"

"A *woman* should place as much emphasis and energy on her career as a man. Rand understands that and that's really all that matters to me."

"Are you so sure he understands? That's what you said when you refused to live with him, but you never saw how unhappy he was, a married man living like a lonely bachelor."

A sharp hiss slipped through Nicole's teeth. She felt the fury threatening to trample her self-control. "I'm sorry, but I don't have time to argue with you about it just now. I promised to meet Rand at the station and I'm late."

"I didn't mean to be arguing with you. It's just that I'm concerned . . . for you both."

"I know, Dee, I know." Nicole braided her fingers through the beige rubber of the phone cord and tried to tell herself that she did know and understand. She said good-bye as smoothly as possible, hung up, then stood frowning at her cord-entwined fingers. The echo of Dee's flat "when you refused to live with him" rang in her ears.

Even after so many years, such a statement had the power to hurt her. It hadn't been like that at all; the decision to live apart for the sake of their respective careers had been mutual, but she'd never been able to convince anyone else of that. Family and friends had been quick to assume she'd demanded Rand accept marriage on her terms. All her defensive pride hadn't shielded her from the pain of their accusations. Hadn't anyone realized how lonely she'd been during those two years? How hard the struggle to sustain her marriage and her career had been?

And now, once again, it appeared she was being viewed as an unnatural wife, as a woman seemingly bent on making her husband miserable. She felt her chest constricting, squeezing painfully. Wasn't there anyone on either side of the family who was on her side?

If only she'd been granted the power of clairvoyance! Had she been able to foresee the ruckus she'd cause among her family, Nicole would never have so casually mentioned to her mother that she and Rand had applied for the same position at the station. The result had been a nightly string of calls from parents, sisters, brothers, even her Aunt Grace in Broken Bow, Nebraska. Each call had been the same. Guarded warnings to Nicole on the peril (or in the case of Aunt Grace, the perfidy) of a wife competing directly against her husband. The consensus of one and all seemed to be that Nicole should give way to the traditional role of a wife and place Rand's career first.

The past two weeks had been a virtual replay of the months following her marriage, when it seemed every relative she and Rand possessed had attempted to convince her to give up her job and join him in Des Moines. Then, Rand had been the balm to ease her hurt, stoutly supporting her decision to stay in Columbia. This time, his support seemed less bracing. She couldn't have said in just what way she felt the lack. He still firmly but politely told those who interfered that it wasn't anyone else's business. Yet, Nicole couldn't shake the feeling that he didn't back her as he had before. She suspected he'd like to add his voice to the family chorus and her doubt heightened her sensitivity to remarks such as Dee's.

From the dining room the chime of the brass ship's clock announced the approach of the new hour. She lurched, cursed, freed her fingers from the phone cord, and grabbed her purse as she dashed for the door. Rand would be waiting, wondering where she was and why she was so late. Careening down the stairs and out into the parking lot, she fumed, first at her interfering sister-in-law, then at her absent husband. Why'd he have to work late tonight? He should have spoken with Dee—after all, she was *his* sister. Let *him* keep the family wolves at bay for a change.

An unexpected jerk on her shoulder halted her in midstep. Her canvas purse splattered on the pavement, yawning open to spill its contents in a tumbling heap. Glaring accusingly at the frayed end of the torn shoulder strap, Nicole bent and hurriedly stuffed her possessions back into her bag. Within the hazy bluish lighting, the glint of a jagged break marring a small round mirror winked at her. Her irritation escalated. That's all she needed—seven years' bad luck. As if things weren't going badly enough already.

By the time she'd backed the sedan out of the carport and onto the street, she had irrationally decided it was all Rand's fault. His fault for staying late to finish work on a special feature series dealing with the Blue Laws, which still restricted Sunday sales in some parts of Missouri, including St. Louis, but which had been repealed elsewhere. She understood his interest in the controversy and his desire to have the series in the can, ready to air next week on the early evening news, but didn't he realize she needed him at home?

An unwanted thought popped into her head. Perhaps he was so anxious to finish the series in order to reinforce the image of his on-camera expertise, to once again impress home viewers and, more importantly, Joe and Lionel. She pushed the petty thought out of her mind, telling herself that he'd done such features before, it was part of his job. He didn't have to prove himself, not with the audience nor with management.

Still, he seemed unusually anxious to get this one on the air. . . .

Their applications had been made simultaneously on the previous Monday. Lionel had accepted them with a noncommittal grunt, a sharp glance from one to the other being his only admission of surprise. Others at the station were more vocal; to them all, she and Rand had presented a united front of silence on the subject. Despite their resolution to talk about it, they'd discussed it only sparingly, cautiously, with the trepidation of crossing a frozen pond labeled DANGER, THIN ICE.

It had taken two full weeks for the first hint of a crack to appear. During a commercial break on this noon's show, Barry had leaned his lanky form on his camera and remarked casually that the show sure would be different without Rand as cohost. Nicole stiffened, pink sheets slipping from her numbed fingers. Hesitating so briefly as to seem not to have hesitated at all, Rand bent and scooped the script from the floor. Handing it to his wife, he turned to face the crew.

"Oh? You know something I don't? Have Joe and Lionel taken you into their confidence?"

The serrated edge to his tone caused more than one mouth to drop open. Like all television programs, *STL* was very much a group effort, with everyone relying on everyone else to get the job done. But even among a crew where a cooperative camaraderie was the norm, Rand's calm temperament was considered remarkable. To hear even a slight acidic note drip from his words shocked those who'd worked with him so closely over the past four years.

Only Nicole didn't react. She was preoccupied with the plunging disappointment, the smothering hostility overwhelming her. She was shocked by how she'd overreacted to Barry's remark—she'd felt as if the studio had toppled in on her. Her stomach clenched. What if Barry *had* known something? How would she feel then?

Barry shuffled back behind camera two. He caught several pairs of eyes still focusing on him. He cleared his throat. "Uh, no. I just assumed—"

"You assumed wrong," broke in Rand, though more kindly now. "There's a lot of people up for that job. They've gotten applications from all over the country. It's too early for speculation of any type."

"Yeah, sure," mumbled Barry.

"Stand by and cue," boomed an unseen, godlike voice from the master control room, and Sharla immediately positioned herself between the cameramen. She pointed to Nicole, then swung her hands to camera one.

Still unreasonably flustered, Nicole fluffed her lines. That, more than anything else, disturbed her. She'd betrayed to everyone there just how much Barry's casual comment had affected her. She'd revealed just how badly she wanted that anchor spot.

Rand had jumped in with a smooth ad-lib and her professional expertise responded to it almost automatically. All was well within seconds, but the incident left her feeling unsettled, a state of mind that Dee's call had unhappily exacerbated.

Of all of Rand's large and uninhibited family—he was the fourth of five children born within seven years—it was his eldest sister Deanna who could most easily ignite the fuse of Nicole's hot temper. Outspoken and opinionated, Dee never hesitated to say bluntly what she felt, and she often criticized Nicole without missing a breath. Nicole wasn't used to receiving such strictures. With a gap of more than eight years between her two brothers and herself, Nicole had grown up being petted and spoiled, treated as something quite special. It had taken years for her to realize that Dee's criticism stemmed from real affection. But that didn't make it sting any less.

By the time she'd parked in KSTL's back lot, Nicole had regained most of her composure. Her faith in Rand was too great to be dented by interfering relatives, niggling suspicions, or even by lingering bruises to her own ego. Whatever happened, they'd agreed to accept it like good sportsmen, and she meant to abide by that agreement.

Though the halls vibrated with the usual flow of business, she felt eerily out of place to be there at such an odd hour. The faces passing by were only faintly familiar; the night crew and cast seemed to change more frequently than their daytime counterparts. But she greeted those she recognized and even paused to peek briefly into the hectically astir newsroom, where lights glared, voices buzzed, and machines clacked. An assistant producer sat at the computer that tapped into all the major newspapers and magazines in the world. A machine next to the UPI and AP wires was spitting out a Laserphoto of the President. Two reporters brushed past her, muttering apologies as they ran to their typewriters. She waved at Craig McCall, then continued on to the subdued hush of her own office. She couldn't help wondering what it would be like to be a part of that vigorously animated scene.

Already late to meet him, she half expected Rand to appear before she reached their office, but instead she entered to find his cubicle vacant. The light above his desk cascaded gently over stacks of papers and tapes, rippling into soft shadows where his tie draped over the back of his chair and his tan suitcoat hung from a wallhook.

Assured he was still somewhere on the premises, Nicole sat down at her own desk and took the opportunity to catch up on the backlog of correspondence. People wrote in with questions, requests, suggestions, and just remarks that they liked the show. Nicole tried to respond to all of it, feeling that anyone who took the time to write deserved a reply, however brief. Occasionally Rand helped out, but she didn't expect much help from the man who in six years had addressed approximately two Christmas cards. "If I'd wanted to be a writer," he always told her with a broad grin, "I'd have been a print journalist, right?" She didn't mind, though, because writing letters was a task she enjoyed. She liked reading what viewers had to say and reaching out to them in return.

She became so immersed in her work, she nearly jumped out of her skin when a silhouette fell over her shoulder. She spun round, exclaiming, "Oh, Rand, you scared the—"

Her breathless admonition was severed into silence by the sight of the man beside her. That broken mirror had already begun to work its unlucky charm.

Frank's beautiful blue eyes shone guilelessly; his perfect smile invited candid confidences. "Sorry, I didn't mean to surprise you."

"I thought you were Randell," she said, faintly reproachful.

"I believe he's locked up in editing booth number three."

Automatically, she glanced at her watch. The late hour startled her. "Still?" she said before she could stop herself.

A hint of speculation passed through the beautiful

blues. Then Frank shrugged. "He didn't get started on any of it until after nine. He got tied up at dinner." His gaze slewed past hers. "But I suppose you expected that."

Not for anything in the world would Nicole have admitted she didn't know what he was talking about. Leaning back in her chair, she looked at him. The corners of her mouth tucked inward; a line creased the space between her heavy brows. Rand called this her "prim" look and it would have made any other man back away. Frank, however, braced against the edge of her desk, stretching his slim legs out to block her entryway, and remarked nonchalantly that he liked her jumpsuit. "Nice color. What is that?"

"Mist-green," she replied, and waited. She knew Frank couldn't care less about her jumpsuit. He had more to say. He wouldn't waste his time with her otherwise. He'd always had the attitude that he couldn't be bothered with anyone in "soft" news.

"Like the ruffles," he drawled. He picked up the top letter, scanned it, and laughed a ghost of a laugh. "This is one viewer you've lost."

"What do you mean?"

"She writes that she watches *STL* because 'Randell Clarke is so charming' and more equally nauseating descriptions."

"What are you implying, Frank? Quit playing games and say whatever it is you have to say." She spoke sharply. At the best of times Frank had an abrasive effect on her, and tonight wasn't the best of times.

The letter fluttered back to the top of the stack. Nicole watched its gradual descent as if viewing it in slow motion. When it landed, the soft plop mimicked the sinking of her heart.

"I just thought," he said at last, "that we could offer each other condolences on being also-rans."

"I don't know what you mean."

"I'm talking about the dinner your hubby had with Korsinski and Pinder, the private dinner that lasted two hours. Let's face it, it's all over but the formalities. Rand didn't wine and dine with Joe and Lionel to talk about the latest presidential candidate to pass through town."

A bitter twist marred the perfection of Frank's mouth. Even more than his harsh words, that twist convinced Nicole he was telling the truth. But still a part of her demanded she deny such a betrayal. She forced herself to focus her gaze on her typewriter, to wave a hand in airy dismissal. "I wouldn't worry about it if I were you, Frank. It's probably some trumped-up bit of gossip to make the rest of us green."

Frank puckered his lips in a quiet whistle. A malicious gleam brightened his narrowed gaze. "So your dear, devoted husband didn't tell you? God, it's amazing how ambition will distort a person. When even Randell Clarke starts deceiving his wife to—"

"I don't find this joke of yours amusing, Frank."

"Sorry to be the one to burst your bubble of marital bliss, Nicole, but I'm not joking. It's true. I saw the three of them at Al's Steak House myself. And I saw them huddled together in the newsroom when they got back. It's a fact, baby. Check it out."

Somehow, she managed a level tone. "Don't you have a newscast to do in a few minutes?"

He steadily scrutinized her, making her acutely uncomfortable, for several unending seconds before he finally straightened. Pushing a hand through his neatly trimmed light brown hair, he said sourly, "I suppose it's okay for you. After all, you're keeping it in the family."

When she was certain he had to be completely out of hearing, Nicole snapped off her typewriter and uttered an obscenity she hadn't even realized she'd known. If what Frank had said was true—and the churning in her stomach left her in little doubt that it was—then why hadn't Rand told her he was going for dinner with Lionel and Joe? Why had he told her he was staying late to work on the feature series? He wouldn't keep something like that from her—would he? Anxious to give him the benefit of the doubt, she decided it must have happened unexpectedly. Lionel had passed him in the hall and invited him along for a meal with the general manager. Naturally he had to accept. It had to be something like that. She'd wait and hear from Rand exactly what had happened before jumping to wild conclusions.

So when Rand stuck his head around the corner and said cheerily, "Hi, beautiful," she met his greeting with a reasonably pleasant "Hi, yourself. All finished with your feature?"

He dumped a set of videotapes on his desk. "All except for getting it onto the proper desk. But that'll wait until tomorrow. For now, I can't wait to get out of here." Yanking his jacket off its hook and grabbing a fistful of silk tie, he ushered her out into the corridor, saying, "God, whoever thinks this is a glamor business ought to put in a twelve-hour day and see just how glamorous it isn't. Were you waiting long?"

"Not too," she answered, avoiding his eyes. "I was late getting here myself. Dee called."

"Oh, no. I'm sorry, sweetheart. Did she do her usual

'it's only because I love you that I'm butting in where I don't belong' routine?"

"Complete with moans, groans, and weary sighs."

"And . . . ?"

"And I told her I didn't have time to argue."

They reached the car. Rand held open the passenger door and gazed down at Nicole as she slid into her seat. "She really does love us both, you know. It's just that to Dee, everything's clear and simple, black-and-white, and when something isn't what she sees as white, she thinks it's her duty to repaint it."

Nicole waited until he was seated on his side of the car before telling him she knew that. "But it doesn't make it any easier to hear her tell me I'm a bad wife."

He leaned over the gearshift and pressed his palms into her cheeks. "Dee's as good as gold, but she doesn't know diddly-do about what makes a good wife. You're a great wife. I say so and that's all that counts."

After kissing her once, hard, he released her to turn his attention to driving. The joy she might have felt in his loving defense of her didn't materialize. Frank's ugly accusation overshadowed all else. She sat stiffly, tensely waiting for him to laugh and say how he'd been carried off to dinner with Joe and Lionel when all he'd wanted to do was finish his tapes. She waited for him to say how boring, how interesting, how amusing his dinner had been. She waited for him to even mention he'd had a dinner.

He didn't. He asked if any other family dragons had called to breathe fire over the phone wires. She told him no, and after a moment he began relating an anecdote about the night cast sound engineer and his attempts to get Eva Baere to go out with him, all of which had thus far ended in comical failure. Nicole heard him speak without listening to what he said. The realization that he wasn't going to say anything about his dinner was slowly sinking in. She was stunned. She could only conclude that he'd known all along about it; that he'd deliberately kept it a secret from her. More, that he'd actually lied to her about why he had to stay late at the station. She fixed her gaze on the unseen view. The ghostly imprint of her reflection wavered on the window, sad and hollow eyed. How could Rand lie to her?

Even as her heartbeat thudded with a sluggish sadness, her blood began to blaze within her veins. How long, she wondered, just how long did he intend to keep stringing her along? "By the way," she cut in when he paused in his story, "should we stop to get you something to eat?"

"I've eaten, thanks. What about you?"

She didn't think she'd be able to answer for the furious pain that was blocking her throat. She managed a brief "I ate." He resumed his story. It occurred to her that he was speaking to cover his guilt and she felt her pain expanding. Each minute of the journey home throbbed by as she sat in aching silence.

As soon as the apartment door clicked shut behind them, however, she rounded on him. For a moment she faltered. Weary lines had etched themselves into his face, emphasizing the narrow width. His generally immaculate hair fell in soft disarray over his brow. The off-white shirt clung with damp wrinkles to his chest. As she hesitated, he tossed his jacket and tie onto the indigo loveseat, rumpled his hair into further dishevelment, and grinned crookedly.

"What a torturous day. I'm beat."

Instantly her rush of sympathy receded. He should be beat—preferably with a frying pan. "That's what those private dinners will do to you. They're so exhausting," she drawled with all the sarcasm she could muster.

He didn't pretend to misunderstand, she had to give him credit for that. "If you're referring to my dinner with Joe and Lionel—"

"Bingo. Bull's-eye," she snapped, feeling that he'd struck the target somewhere in the vicinity of her solar plexus. It was a wonder she could still stand. She clenched her hands together and glared at him.

"It was hardly what you could call private," he said calmly. "We ate at Al's, in the middle of the dinner crowd."

Her anger soared. How could he remain so calm? He'd betrayed her, lied to her, and now he placidly admitted it! She wanted to shake him until his back molars came loose. "Don't nitpick," she said. "Just tell me why you had to lie about it."

"I didn't lie to you, Nicole." He glanced around, as if to orient himself to his surroundings. She thought he was stalling and said so. He sighed. "Come here. Sit with me," he coaxed. He moved to the loveseat.

"I don't feel like sitting, thank you. You don't think it's a lie to tell me you're staying late to work when you're actually going to Al's with the men who just coincidentally will decide who gets the anchor job?"

Her voice had risen sharply. She'd heard it escalating but felt helpless to stop it. The shrill piercing of her heart had to find release somehow.

"Think we ought to check on the wineglasses?"

Usually that was the sort of remark guaranteed to break the flow of her temper. Usually. But this wasn't their usual sort of quarrel and Nicole refused to react in the expected manner. She flapped her hands and declared, "This is one time you aren't going to humor me out of my anger, Randell Clarke. This is one time you're going to give me the satisfaction of an explanation."

"Somehow, honey, I don't think my explanation is going to satisfy you."

"Try me."

"Lionel wanted to discuss doing a documentary in conjunction with the elections this year. It just happened that we discussed it over dinner."

She wanted to believe him. She needed to believe him. When he patted the cushion beside him, she slowly crossed and perched herself at the edge of it. She was more aware than she wanted to be of the close proximity of Rand's knee to her own. She could sense the weariness in him, in the way he sagged into the cushions, but she refused to respond to it. This time she wouldn't permit him to tease or tempt or touch her into forgetting why she was upset. This time she'd respond only to a rational excuse and a sincere apology. She desperately wanted to receive both.

"Why didn't you tell me about this?" she asked in a quiet little voice that begged for reassurance.

"I knew you'd misconstrue it," he said, and she was suddenly angry all over again.

"So you'd rather go out on the sly, sneaking around to meet Joe and Lionel without my finding out, is that it? Didn't you stop to think how I'd construe that? Well, let me tell you just what construction I put on it. It looks to me as if you met them to discuss the anchor job and you didn't want me to find out about it."

"I haven't been given that job," he began, but stopped as she leaped to her feet.

"I don't care about the job! That's not the point, Rand!

The point is you didn't tell me about this so-called documentary and you deliberately tried to keep me from finding out about your meeting with Joe and Lionel. It's the lying and the sneaking—"

"The devious, shifty, two-timing," he threw in helpfully.

"Go ahead and make jokes. It's not funny."

"Maybe not, but you are. You should see how red your face is turning. Any minute now steam'll pour right out of your ears."

Steam nearly did. Nicole had heard of being blind with rage, but she'd never before experienced it. She gritted her teeth until her jaws ached to keep from shouting at him. She felt betrayed and hurt and let it show in every rigid line of her stance.

"I'm serious, Rand. *This* is serious. I'm not talking about your failure to take out the garbage. I'm talking about your failure to confide in me."

"Is it written somewhere that we have to tell one another every little thing we're planning to do?"

She ignored his placating half smile. "Just for the record, when did you plan to tell me about this? When it was announced you're going to replace Craig? Or not at all?"

Rand came to his feet. "Look, I'm tired and I don't feel up to coaxing you into believing me. But just for the record, we talked about the documentary, nothing else. Lionel knew I wanted to do some producing, so he gave me first shot at it. Joe came along because he was hungry and lonely—his wife is visiting their daughter in Terre Haute this week. Now you can either accept that and come to bed with me, or you can stay up and steam. It's up to you."

He waited a long tense moment before pivoting and

striding off down the hall. She waited even longer before switching the lights off and following him. "What about our rule?" she demanded as she charged into the bedroom.

He paused in the act of turning down the bedcovers to look over his shoulder at her. "What about it?"

"Didn't we agree never to go to bed until an argument was settled?"

"I thought this was settled."

Her hands curled into tight little fists. "Nothing's been settled and you know it."

"You asked for an explanation. I gave it to you. I can't help it if you're unhappy with it."

This cool, remote man wasn't her Rand. It was some stranger standing there beside her bed, telling her he couldn't help it if he'd made her unhappy. How could she talk to a stranger? She drew a deep breath that rattled her lungs. "It's not the explanation that has me unhappy. It's you. It's not understanding why you kept the whole thing a secret from me. It's not knowing whether or not to believe you."

The hint of a rueful smile tugged at his mouth. "I'd tell you to believe me, honey, but you'd probably doubt that too. I admit I erred by not telling you I'd be going out with Lionel tonight, but I didn't do so for any nefarious reason. It was only to keep you from thinking just what you have been thinking. Admit it, even if I'd told you about the dinner, you'd have suspected the reasons for it. I know that suspicious mind of yours, I know how it works, and I thought I was saving us both some grief. My mistake."

Slowly, almost unwillingly, her hands unfurled. She averted her eyes from the power of his crooked smile. She didn't want to be charmed into believing him. She still didn't know what she believed. The story smelled as wholesome as week-old fish. Yet Rand had never lied to her before. That is, never before tonight. She couldn't ignore the fact that the half truth he'd told her tonight had been a lie of sorts. She toyed with the fluted ruffles of her jumpsuit and felt miserable.

Rand finished folding the spread into a neat rectangle at the foot of the bed. He shed his clothes and hung them over a mahogany valet she'd given him last Christmas. The simple action filled her with sadness. She felt as if she were watching him through the wrong end of a pair of binoculars; the view was distorted and deceptive. He seemed unapproachably far away. He climbed into bed and stretched, his skin glowing in the muted light. He was all muscle and masculinity and more than a little spell-binding. "Coming?" he asked.

She started. Mechanically she loosened the buttons down the front of her jumpsuit, then stepped out of the garment. It amazed her that she could actually move to the closet, select a hanger, and drape the jumpsuit on it as if everything were perfectly normal. Nothing at all was normal. Not the way her heart was twisting erratically in her chest. Not the way her lungs were pressing each breath out past that solid lump in her throat. And certainly not the way this rift in her marriage was widening with every second that ticked past.

She could feel Rand's gaze on her while she donned a thin nylon teddy. It made her feel vulnerable. In defense she stoked up the flagging embers of her hostility. Why should she be the one to feel sad and defenseless? He was the one in the wrong. He was the one who'd kept a secret from her, who'd as much as said he didn't care if it made her unhappy. Self-righteous wrath returned to her in full force. As she got into bed beside him, she said acidly, "Don't expect anything tonight."

"I wasn't," he said.

"Good," she said, and flipped onto her side.

The bed shook gently as he stretched to turn off the light in the headboard, swayed slightly as he slid down into place. The darkness wrapped around Nicole, but brought her no warmth. Ice ran in her veins and a solid block of it encased her heart. She waited for Rand to say something, to apologize, to reach out and kiss or tease her into forgiving him. Instead the night grew cooler, the hours longer, and the silence deeper.

CHAPTER FIVE

"Excuse me," said Nicole politely as she reached past Rand for the hair dryer.

He turned off his shaver and stepped out of her way. The sudden silence reverberated loudly. The small room seemed to shrink, the space separating them reduced to fractions of an inch. "Would you like to have this mirror?" he asked, his voice politely matching hers.

"No, thank you. The one in the bedroom will do just as well." She grabbed the dryer and escaped. Even that brief exchange had seemed suffocating; she didn't know how she was going to get through a whole day of being around him.

As she dried and styled her hair, she justified her refusal to forgive Rand by the mere fact that he had not asked for forgiveness. He hadn't apologized, he hadn't even wanted to discuss the matter. He'd broken their long-standing commitment not to let a day end with an argument unsettled between them. During an interminably long and restless night, she'd told herself repeatedly—and very convincingly—that she didn't care whether or not the purpose of that dinner had been to offer Rand the anchor spot. That he'd tried to deceive her about it was what hurt so unbearably.

And now, of course, there was the added pain of this too-civil detachment.

He came in, his shapely form well displayed by the fluffy mauve towel carelessly draped over his hips. It took all her willpower not to fling her body into his arms and cry. She reminded herself that he was the one who'd started this, he was the one who should make the first move. She turned her back to him as she dressed. She donned a white sundress with a crimson belt and a short-waisted red jacket to match, all the while trying to ignore the soft roll of drawers opening and closing, the hushed *plop* of the towel hitting the floor, the quiet rustle of clothes, the rasp of a zipper. She waited until he had moved back to the dresser to knot his tie before entering the closet to get her shoes. A muted lime scent lingered within the cubicle, teasing her, tormenting her. She thrust her feet into red pumps and hurried out to the kitchen.

The rousing aroma of fresh coffee permeated the air, but failed to stimulate her. Usually Nicole felt enlivened by the invigorating smell, by the glint of morning light boucing off the copper-bottomed pots hanging over the stove, by the gleam of polished chrome on the appliances. Today her senses were too dulled to appreciate any of it.

She couldn't even enjoy the miniature rainbows dappling the sink and walls. The bright streams of light whisking through the stained-glass sun catchers scattered over the window seemed to mock her with memories of happier times. The blues of the owl Rand had given her for "wise-ly" deciding to marry him. The lavenders of an iris he'd said reminded him of her eyes. The reds and greens of a bouquet of balloons that had marked her thirtieth birthday ("You stay as young as you want to," he'd told her). She looked away from the cheery prisms. The memories hurt too much.

Within minutes Rand joined her. They stood side-by-side at the small counter as they washed down a fistful of vitamins with cups of grapefruit juice. Torn between her stubborn will and her bruised ego, Nicole wavered between taking action and waiting. Deep down she kept thinking any minute now he would admit he'd been wrong, tease her into a smile and kiss her soundly. But minute after minute crawled wordlessly by. With each that passed, the gap between them stretched ever wider.

"Ready?" he finally said.

She set down her unfinished coffee. "Yes," she said. The single syllable sounded cool and clipped. She checked her reflection in the shine of the toaster, collected her purse, and followed him out. She clung to the belief that this strain couldn't go on much longer. It wasn't like Rand to be so distant. Soon he would talk to her, she was certain of it.

The smile that passed between them was warmly intimate. The brief touch of hands sweetly loving.

"This is Randell Clarke—"

"And this is Nicole Clarke—"

"Thank you for joining us—"

"And have a great afternoon."

The ceiling full of huge track lights slowly dimmed. Sharla nodded and pulled the headset from her short cinnamon hair. Ted and Barry lowered each camera to its triangular base. Nicole unclipped the microphone from the lapel of her muslin jacket and stood. She shook the wrinkles from her candy-striped dress. One of the sleeves of her jacket slid down her arm; she rolled it back up to her elbow. She hoped no one noticed how clumsy her fingers were. She was still trembling from the lingering poignancy of his fleeting touch. . . .

She'd thought she knew him. To discover she did not pierced with an acutely bitter accuracy. She'd thought—no, she'd *known*—he would crook a smile at her and cajole her into accepting his apology. She'd thought the passing of one night with a dispute in bed between them like an old-fashioned bundling roll was an aberration, a never-to-be-repeated abnormality. Yet here they were with yet another night of frigid silence between them and still no thaw in sight.

Beside her, Rand sipped from a can of cola he pulled out from under the coffee table. Without looking at him she walked past the cameramen to a row of chairs at the back of the studio.

"Did you enjoy the show, Mrs. Shanley?" she asked a middle-aged woman sitting there. As part of a promotion for an upcoming crafts festival, the woman had been on the show to demonstrate her method of quilting. Following her segment, she had stayed to watch the remainder of the program.

"Oh, my, yes," she said now, obviously excited by the attention. "It's been such fun for me. I enjoy your show so much. You and Mr. Clarke are so perfect together."

A hand slid round Nicole's waist, startling her. "Yes, we are," said Rand.

"It was a real privilege for me to be on *STL Noon,*" gushed Mrs. Shanley.

He smiled. Nicole knew he smiled by the giddy glow that suffused the older woman's face in response. She wanted to jab her elbow into his ribs. He couldn't spare an off-camera smile for her, no, sir, but for everyone else he dropped smiles like apple blossoms in April.

"We couldn't do the show without guests like you," he said with what Nicole considered nauseating charm.

"Oh, but it's the two of you that make the show worth watching. Really, the love you two have is a thrill to see."

"Thank you," put in Nicole quickly. She couldn't tolerate another second of this. She stepped out of Rand's light clasp and took her guest's arm. "Shall I show you the way out?"

Crossing over fat black cables that snaked over the bare wood floor, they passed the darkened newscast set. "Is that where they do the TV-7 news?" Mrs. Shanley inquired. Nicole answered affirmatively, which released a flood of commentary from the other woman as they exited through a maze of wood and wires. Nicole made no effort to stem the flow; it was as much as she could to insert the occasional "Umm," and "Oh, yes?" She scarcely even listened. She was wondering why Rand had put on that little demonstration of marital affection. For public image? Or to tell her something?

At the reception area Nicole bid her guest good-bye, then paused as Ginny greeted her. "You two were great today," said the receptionist, nodding toward the television built into the wall beside her desk. "As always," she added.

"Thanks," said Nicole automatically. If Rand were only half as miserable as she'd been the last two days, then surely he was trying to make amends. Surely he couldn't bear the thought of another day, another night like yesterday's. Surely he—with a start, she realized Ginny had spoken.

"Wish you'd tell me how you've managed to keep the flame going after all this time," the receptionist had sighed wistfully. "How long have you been married?"

"Six years," replied Nicole leadenly. "Well, almost six. Six this summer."

"Must be nice. After two, I can hardly get Billy to look at me, much less look at me so lovingly."

The unwitting irony of Ginny's words stung sharply. In other people's eyes, Rand might still seem to look at her lovingly, but from her view, it was a facade, an expert bit of playacting. The hope that had been fluttering since he'd assured their guest they were perfect together died abruptly. Of course, that had only been for effect. There'd been no loving looks, no tender touches last night. Out of the public eye, there had been only unapproachable silence.

All her worst forebodings had been realized in a nightmare of distance between them. At work, deadly polite conversation bridged the breach, but it was a bridge of rope shaking in a high wind. How long would it be until the rope snapped?

For the umpteenth time she asked herself how the hell it had happened. No answer conveniently materialized. All she knew was that the longer it went on, the harder it became for either to end it. She saw them drifting further and further apart, but felt helpless to buck the current. Because Rand had always been the one to unbend, the one to placate and pacify, she'd expected him to do so now. The fact that he hadn't added to her belief that he was clearly in the wrong, made her unwilling to take the first step toward closing the rift. And yet she wanted nothing more than to clear the air between them, to cleanse and purify their tainted relationship.

If only he'd apologized to her that first night. If only she'd accepted his explanation and let it go at that. If only they'd talked about it yesterday morning. If only that damn job weren't standing between them. Her footsteps slowed as she neared her office. If only . . . Her life seemed filled with if onlys.

A vending machine sandwich, a pack of barbecue chips, and a cola waited atop her desk. Again hope bloomed, only to wither as Rand spoke in the cool, remote tone he'd used with her these last two days. "If you don't want ham for lunch, I'll take it and you can have this pastrami."

"Ham's fine," she replied woodenly. So much for the perfect couple, she thought as she ripped the packet of chips open. Perfect in public, maybe. In private they were a decidedly imperfect couple. She stuck a chip in her mouth, chewed, and swallowed. The acrid salt was all she tasted. They hadn't always been so imperfect. In the past she'd often thought they were as close to perfection as she'd ever hope to be. She licked salt from her lips and came to a decision. This couldn't go on any longer. She couldn't bear it anymore. Whether she was in the right or wrong didn't matter. Their future did.

Swinging abruptly to face him, she exclaimed, "Rand, we've got to talk."

The aisle yawned between them. He slowly turned in his chair to gaze at her. A certain wariness stole into his eyes. "What about?"

"Us. I think we've—"

"Sorry to interrupt your lunch," said Eva Baere as she stuck her head in the door, "but the Lion's snarling for you, Randell. He wants you on the double. Did I miss some excitement on your program or something?"

He shrugged, set down his sandwich, and dusted his fingers on the cellophane wrapper. "What's there to miss? Excitement isn't standard fare on *STL*." His chair swayed as he came lithely to his feet. He paused by the door and turned to look at his wife. He offered her a tilted smile, the kind she'd been longing to see. "Hold that thought, whatever it was. I'll be back as soon as I can. Provided the Lion doesn't eat me for lunch."

Eva stepped aside to let him pass, then came in and leaned against Nicole's desk. "So what happened on your show?"

"Nothing. Same old routine."

"Rand didn't insult a guest?" She sounded disappointed, but behind her glasses, her eyes sparkled merrily.

"No, nothing. It was just a show like all the other shows." Nicole sounded dejected; her eyes didn't sparkle at all. Had fate sent her a message by sending Eva to stop her from talking to Rand?

Never in her wildest imaginings would she have believed it to be this difficult to reach out to him. She'd always been able to confide in him so easily, about everything. And up to now he'd shared all his thoughts with her. Now he barely shared the time of day. Even the competition for anchor couldn't explain their current lack of communication. Once before they'd faced a conflict between their careers and their relationship and they'd worked that out together.

But then, pointed out a nagging voice she'd rather not have listened to, Rand had wanted her success as much as she had. He could not want her to succeed this time. If she succeeded, he failed. They weren't teammates, they were rivals—and it was breaking them apart.

"I guess it is pretty unlikely, Rand insulting someone. Still, Lionel seemed more than usually ferocious. May I?" Reaching even as she spoke, Eva took a couple of chips and nibbled delicately at one. "Rumor has it Joe's about to make an announcement. Do you think—"

"I don't have time to waste on gossip! I've got work to do!" erupted Nicole on a note so shrill, the clack of the typewriter in the cubicle beyond hers stopped momentarily. She could visualize the speculation crossing Doug Sims's face and mentally cringed. When the sportscaster's typing resumed, she apologized to Eva for her outburst.

"It's okay." Eva managed to look at once engagingly unrepentant and sincerely apologetic. "I shouldn't have been so nosy, but you know how it is. Reporters have inquiring minds and all that. I just thought if Joe'd made a decision, there might be a connection to Rand's being summoned by Lionel."

That thought had occurred to Nicole, too, but she wouldn't admit it. Instead she said she really thought it was too soon to expect a decision from Joe and turned to the lunch she had no desire to eat. Eva moved on to her own desk. Nicole heard the low mumble of conversation from the next cubicle and knew Eva was telling Doug what had triggered her small explosion. They'd no doubt attribute it to professional jealousy. She wanted the job, she couldn't deny it. Nor could she deny that it pricked her pride when everyone else assumed Rand would get the position. She knew she was a good newswoman. She knew she was as deserving of the anchor position as he. If she was totally honest with herself, she had to admit jealousy played a part in her current unhappiness.

She tried to think if there had been anything on any of their recent programs to have Lionel raging at Rand. It was amazingly difficult for her to even remember the programs they'd done. Though she generally got enthusiastic before each program, once the show was over, it was over. She completely forgot about it. After so many years it was little more than a mechanical routine. For her to remember one, there had to be an exceptional guest or some topic that stuck in her mind. She tried, but couldn't recall anything that would have upset the news director. She concluded he wanted Rand to discuss something other than *STL Noon.*

Naturally, the conclusion depressed her. Even though she told herself it really *was* too soon to expect a decision, even though she told herself it must be the elections documentary Rand had mentioned, she didn't believe it for a second. She was certain it could only be about the anchor position. All the original hurt and anger over his deception returned, amplified by the discord still clashing between them, and she felt grateful to Eva for her timely interruption. She had nothing to apologize to him for!

When Rand reappeared, she pretended not to notice him. It was exceedingly difficult, given the fact he stood right behind her and toyed with the ends of her hair. The alluring lime of his after-shave floated on the air. The heat of his body warmed her back and the power of his presence weakened her resistance.

"Before I was so abruptly summoned away, you started to say something. What was it?"

His fingers trailed under her hair, grazing her nape. Her shoulders tensed. A shiver fluttered down the length of her spine and she jerked away from his reach. She couldn't allow herself to be placated by him like this. She had every right to expect a full apology first. "Nothing," she said unsteadily. "What was Lionel upset about?"

He studied her for a long moment before replying. "He wasn't upset. You know how he gets when he's harried."

"So what did he want?" she asked, all the while damning him for making her ask. She didn't want to beg to be told he'd been offered the position.

"He just wanted to tell me the documentary's been given the go-ahead from higher up. I'm to work out a budget and let him know what crew I want."

She couldn't meet his gaze. She didn't have to. She could feel the intensity of it.

"I'd like you to help me with this," he said, "if you've got the time."

"I'll think about it," she said slowly.

He placed his weight on her chair, tilting it back until she was forced to look at him. She almost didn't recognize him. His face was cold and set and tensely controlled. If it were someone else, she'd believe he was about to explode with fury. But Rand didn't lose his temper like that . . . did he?

He did. "This should convince you I was telling you the truth about that dinner," he said sharply. "What hurts me is that you have to be convinced. My telling you should have been enough for you."

"That's not fair!" she cried in a harsh whisper. "You deliberately kept your meeting with Lionel a secret from me. What was I to think when you not only met with him, but went out for a dinner with the general manager, and didn't tell me about it? Oh, I believe you about the documentary, you don't have to include me in it to prove anything to me. It's the other lie that hurts me."

"*Other* lie?"

For just a flash, he looked as if strangling her with his bare hands would give him supreme pleasure. She ran the tip of her tongue over her lips and again decided she'd have to apologize. One of them had to, and from the expression on his face, it was obvious it wasn't going to be Rand, not this time. She opened her mouth to speak.

"Ah, we're in luck. The very people we're looking for," chirped a snappy young voice.

Both twisted around to gape at the speaker smiling brightly from the entryway. In canary-yellow slacks and green plaid jacket, Marvin Gederos outshone any of the studio lights. Clothes were Marvin's way to make a mark, for in every other respect he was eminently forgettable. His face was unremarkably pleasant, his thick, drab hair was cropped neatly short, and his voice was a dull monotone. Despite all this, or perhaps because of it, he was the station's top-selling advertising man.

A heavyset stranger stood beside Marvin, looking uncertainly at them. Marvin caught the look and gestured reassuringly. "Randell, Nicole, I'd like you to meet Harold Westerman. Harry's the proud owner of the Westerman Discount Furniture stores throughout the metropolis, and I'm happy to say he's joined the channel seven family of advertisers. As you know, Harry, the Clarkes are the hosts of our *STL Noon* show."

Nicole worked her open mouth into a happy-to-meet-you smile. Rand released her chair to take hold of Mr. Westerman's hand.

"I've been showing Harry around the station," explained Marv, "but thought the two of you could do a better job of telling him how a show like yours is put together."

"It would be a pleasure," said Rand. "Although this is

where we write the script, the real action takes place in the studio, so I suggest we begin there. Shall we?" He spread the charm of his smile around to include his wife, then held out his hand to her.

She stared at it. She knew the smooth strength of that palm, those long fingers. She knew what delight that hand could give. She knew, and she ached inside.

He wiggled his fingers impatiently. She placed her hand within his and stood. They toured first the master control room, with its wall of television screens, bank of telephones, and vast panel of illuminated buttons. Later, in the studio, he tightened his hold on her, threading his fingers with hers. He spoke easily as he pointed out the sets, the TelePrompTer, the cameras, to Mr. Westerman. And throughout it all Nicole wondered whether Rand meant what his hand was saying or if it was merely for show. Was he preserving the image of them as a happy couple or was he attempting to preserve their marriage?

When they left the studio, Harold asked if he could have their autographs. "For my wife," he hastily added and they exchanged an amused glance. It was the closest Nicole had felt to Rand in days. A great welling of hope sprang up. It grew as the amusement in his gaze deepened to affection.

As she signed her name she caught sight of her watch and yelped. "I'm sorry, but I've got to run. I've got some filming to do. It was a pleasure to meet you, Mr. Westerman." She turned to Rand and put everything she couldn't say into her look, her smile. "I'll meet you at home, just as soon as I've got Mama's in the can."

"You mean down the tube, don't you?" he teased.

She flashed a happy grin. It had seemed an age since he'd teased her about anything, and this was a special joke between them. The night they'd gone to Mama's, she'd decided to spotlight it on her "Gateway Nightlife" feature. Rand had been vehemently opposed to it. "It'll ruin it," he'd said. "It'll draw the trendy and the tourists and then Mama's will remodel to upgrade its image and pretty soon it won't be any different from any other restaurant on the Hill."

"Pessimist." She laughed. "I think Mama's will always be unique. And you've got to admit it's a natural. Mama will make a terrific interview."

"You wait," he'd said in a voice of doom, and she had laughed again.

Feeling cheered by his referral to this happier memory, Nicole scooped up her purse and notepad and set off to round up her crew. Ted and the soundman were waiting for her in the commissary, surrounded by a heap of empty candy wrappers and cigarette butts. Telling them she wanted to refresh her makeup, she agreed to meet them out at the van.

The reflection she saw in the mirror of the ladies' room was almost that of a stranger. The dark smudges beneath her eyes emphasized their pale color and brought into sharp focus the toll the breach with Rand had taken.

She closed her eyes and indulged in a gratifying recollection of the feel of Rand's fingers twined with hers. She allowed herself to believe that the rupture was healed and imagined how it would be tonight; the wonder of his touch and kiss and sweet, sweet love. A pleasurable tingle rushed through her midriff. She opened her eyes and found a new glow in them.

She finished dusting her cheeks, nose, and chin with powder and left. As she was crossing the parking lot, a blue Corvette zoomed into her path. She sprang out of the way, cursing under her breath. Her oath deepened in color as the car slowed to a stop. The last thing she wanted was another buddy-to-buddy chat with Frank Walters.

"Hi," he called out as she attempted to walk past his car.

"Hello, Frank. Good-bye, Frank."

The car crept along, keeping pace with her. He leaned out his window. "I've got to hand it to you, Nicole, you're one helluva good sport."

"Thank you," she said, and kept walking. She counted the cars to the van. Ten until she reached it. About nine too many.

"It takes a lot to put in an application for appearances' sake, knowing you aren't even going to be considered."

She stopped. She didn't want to, but her feet seemed to have made the decision on their own. The Corvette also stopped. Frank leaned farther out the window. Sunlight jumped over his reflector sunglasses, and Nicole saw herself staring at him in angry bewilderment.

"I suppose Rand told you there's no chance they'll hire a woman. Craig dropped the word in my ear, and implied Rand's known right from the first. Of course, Rand denied it when I asked him. He even denied discussing the job at all when he went to dinner with Joe and Lionel, but I expected that."

"They talked about a documentary on the elections," she corrected automatically. "Rand's going to produce it."

"Yeah, sure."

Telling herself not to listen to him didn't stop the clamor of outrage, hurt, and a dozen different emotions. Most of all she'd have liked to flatten Frank with his damn sports car. Instead she forced her feet to start moving.

"Good night, Frank," she said again with a brief nod of dismissal.

"I'd wondered why a sharp woman like Eva hadn't applied. She must have known—"

"I've got work to do," she broke in sharply, and hastened her steps. It seemed to take her forever to reach the van. She climbed into the passenger seat and slammed the door, trying to slam the sight and sound of Frank Walters out of her mind. She should have known better than to listen to him. He was like a viper, that man. His poison was insidiously effective. And she didn't know the antidote.

Already new doubts were spilling forth. Was it true? Was she tilting at windmills? Was her application, in fact, not even being considered? And if so, had Rand known about it? Had he known and not said anything? Was this another secret he was keeping to "spare" her?

She directed Ted to the Hill and, once at Mama's, competently did her job. She got a good two-minute feature—Mama had been as delightful as she'd known he'd be—but Nicole took no joy in it. Frank's venom was working its way through her veins all the way to her heart.

When the men dropped her off at her apartment building, she climbed the stairs slowly. She was determined to put Frank's words out of her head. It didn't really matter if he'd told the truth or not. Nothing mattered but getting her derailed marriage back on track.

It seemed that Rand had the same objective in mind. As she entered, he greeted her with a warmth reminiscent of the early days of their marriage, when separation inspired their greetings with an intense fervor. Her brightly colored skirt swirled about her legs, the hem of her jacket flapped, as he swept her up into his arms and swung her lightly into the air.

"Hi, honey," he murmured into the glossy fan of her hair. "How'd it go?"

"Is it true a woman wasn't ever going to be considered for anchor in the first place?"

She clamped her mouth shut, but it was too late. Despite all her resolutions not to ask it, the question had flown from her lips. Though she wished otherwise, she couldn't take it back.

He lowered her slowly to her feet. Her skirt hung limply; his arms fell away from around her waist. "Where did you hear something like that?"

"Frank Walters."

"And you believed him?"

"No. That's why I'm asking you."

"What makes you think I'd know?"

She looked down. Her fingers curled around her notepad. The knuckles were turning white. "Do you?"

The thundering beat of her heart drowned out the low drone of the unwatched television. Seconds ticked by with agonizing slowness. Finally she was compelled to look at him. She glanced up, then wished she hadn't. The loving welcome had vanished, replaced by the guarded mask she'd come to hate. But when he spoke, he sounded calm enough.

"That's the second time today you've made me want to rattle your teeth loose."

"But did you—"

"Don't say it, Nicole," he interrupted. "If you don't know me enough to know I'd have told you if I knew, I don't want to hear about it."

All her pent-up emotions burst forth in one mighty

explosion. "How would I know what you'd do? You haven't been acting like yourself at all! You don't talk to me, you don't tell me things, you go sneaking around—"

"I think that subject's worn a bit thin. I've explained—"

"You call that an explanation? The old I-did-it-for-your-sake routine went out with the horse and buggy."

"If you plan to carry that around to wave under my nose for the rest of our lives, you'll have to excuse me. I don't feel like hearing it just now." He turned on his heel and strode toward the dining room.

Looking past his shoulder, she could see the wineglasses and unlit candles suggesting an intimate dinner to come. "Planning a seduction, were you?" she asked tartly, storming after him. "Is that how you were going to ease my letdown?"

He halted suddenly and she crashed into his back. She jumped back a step as he spun sharply round. He looked her up and down, leisurely assessing her while she ground her teeth in fury.

"Actually," he drawled, "I'd planned to ease something else altogether. Are you interested?"

A long breath whistled between her teeth. She stiffened. "Not with you, I'm not."

He flinched, but almost instantly recovered. "That suits me perfectly. In fact, I'll spare you my presence altogether. I'll move out to the sofa."

"Good. Great. Nothing would please me more. I'll even be happy to help you."

"There's no need to put yourself out."

"Oh, it's a pleasure."

He pivoted and she instantly did likewise. In synchronization they marched together to the linen closet. Rand yanked sheets and a blanket from the top shelf and tossed them into Nicole's arms. She whirled and stamped back to the living room. In a blur of scarlet-and-indigo, Indian print cushions hurled to the floor. Posts thumped heavily as she hauled the sofa seat out to unfold the bed. The mattress curled, resisting her attempts to spread the sheets over it.

"I thought ladies didn't use language like that," Rand said as he came up behind her, his arms overflowing with pillows.

"Do you think you have enough pillows?" she immediately snipped. "One is generally considered sufficient."

He dumped them onto the loveseat. "You should talk. At least I don't have to carry the same damn satin pillow wherever I go. You're worse than that cartoon kid with the blanket."

She straightened and glared at him across the width of the sofa bed. "I sleep better on that particular pillow, that's all."

"And I sleep better with more than one."

"Fine. I'm sorry I said anything," she said, sounding as sorry as a clanging riverboat bell.

"Are you?" he asked, abruptly quiet.

The somber hush of his question deflated her swelling temper. She stood immobile while the tension drained from her. Rand's brown hair was gently mussed, his narrow face was shadowed with weariness. The muted lamplight tinted his cream polo shirt with a peach glow and washed the dark streaks out of his faded blue jeans. This was the Randell Clarke only she saw. This wasn't the immaculate host of *STL,* nor the energetic feature reporter on the night cast. This was *her* Rand. Her husband. The man she loved.

"Yes," she whispered.

"So am I."

A stillness settled over them, neither seeming to dare moving for fear of breaking the delicate thread now binding them. The quarrel seemed silly now. As if Rand would ever sleep on the sofa! Even the last two unendurable nights, he'd lain in bed beside her. A corner of one sheet still twisted within Nicole's fingers. She released it with a sighing laugh. "This was a pretty ridiculous argument, wasn't it?"

"This was a pretty ridiculous week."

His rueful smile squeezed her heart. She glanced down. She wanted him to leap across the bed and take her into his arms. She wanted him to kiss her with unbridled passion, to make love to her with the full force of his being, to love away her heartaches.

Instead Rand aimlessly plumped a pillow and asked if she'd eaten. Thinking she didn't care if she never ate again, she listlessly said no. It seemed an eternity before he discarded the pillow, before he finally spoke. "Are you hungry—or would you rather go to bed?"

"Bed," she said, and waited without daring to breathe.

He reached over the sofa and took her hand. She looked up. Grooves indented beside his mouth, dispelling the harshness from his face. "Me too," he said, and pulled her down onto the curling mattress.

CHAPTER SIX

The mattress groaned beneath their toppling weight. They fell together, legs tangled, arms entwined. For an eternal heartbeat they hesitated within the soft glow of light.

Then his lips were in her hair and his hands were everywhere. From shoulder to spine to hip, his hands swept over her, seeking, demanding, giving. Hot and urgent need filled her wherever he touched. She shuddered with the force of it. Gripping him tightly, she pressed wild kisses on his ear, his neck, his jaw. Their mouths met, clung in desperation.

Somewhere far beneath the raging of her pulse, the quivering of her nerves, Nicole recognized the despair within their explosion of passion. She realized this was really a frenetic attempt to destroy the barriers rising between them. Her turbulent yielding was born of this emotional need.

She tugged impatiently on his shirt, but he didn't respond. He was immersed in his exploration of her. He thrust his hands beneath the loose muslin jacket and skimmed lightly over her bare back. He found the zipper of her dress; the rasp as he lowered it resounded over their mingling breaths. His fingers danced down the ridge of her spine and she moaned.

The need to be part of him, to demolish the division menacing them, compelled her to reckless haste. With a forceful shove, she pushed him away. He looked at her in dazed bewilderment until he saw her sit upright and begin to shrug out of her jacket. Renewed desire darkened his gaze and he stood, yanking his shirt off in the process.

Clothing flew in all directions. The full skirt of her dress billowed like a candy-striped umbrella on its way to the floor. The denim of his jeans cascaded in a puddle of washed-out blue. Hose, panties, briefs, all lay in a heap together. Free of the confines of her clothes, Nicole lay on her back and raised her arms to him.

He sank against her, flattening her breasts with the weight of his chest, pressing his hips into hers. She restlessly ran her hands over the familiar textures of him, the firm smoothness of his chest, the solid musculature of his stomach, the rough rasp of his legs. It was as if she could not reassure herself of the reality of him. He was there, in her arms, kissing her, loving her, but the comfort she sought was missing.

Impatience to find the solace she so intensely needed overwhelmed her. She dug her fingers into his back. She raised her hips, thrusting against him. She tensely arched. "Now, please, now," she begged.

He obliged her. But she wasn't fully ready. Despite her attempt to, she couldn't repress her gasp of pain. He stopped, began to pull away.

"No, please, I need you," she whispered.

"You're not ready. I don't want to hurt you. Let me—"

"Now, Rand, please."

Perhaps he couldn't sense the true nature of her need. Perhaps he couldn't feel her compelling urgency to bond with him, to renew the bond of their marriage with the fusion of their bodies. She didn't know. She only knew that when he continued to hesitate, she wrapped her legs around him and pushed.

He delayed only a second more. And then he was hers completely.

She cried out, but whether from pain or pleasure, she didn't know. She didn't care. All that mattered to her was the fulfillment of their union. To be one with Rand, to be part of him, to have him be part of her, that was what mattered. Praying the love linking them together would be strengthened, she shifted her body to the pulsation of his.

Sweat dampened his hair, his chest, his back. His breath labored over her cheek. His muscles strained. His body tightened. His rhythm slowed, and finally he lay still atop her.

Beyond his shoulder, the golden circle of light spread over the ceiling, gradually dissolving into deep shadows in the corners. She stared at it.

Rand lifted his head. Threads of amber glowed in his hair. "I'm sorry, Coley. Did I hurt you very much?"

Her black hair glossed the pillow as she shook her head. It wasn't a lie, really. The physical hurt had been fleeting, a barely remembered fraction in time. The hurt that was crushing down within her, that was a hurt of her own making. Expectations usually lead to disappointments, after all.

He caught hold of a sable strand. He let it ripple through his fingers. "You didn't enjoy it," he stated flatly.

"That's not true," she managed.

"If you'd only let me—"

"Rand, darling, I wanted you. It's not your fault if I hurried you too much. I enjoyed it anyway. I did."

He rolled away from her. She felt the loss of him deeply. The chill rising on her skin was symbolic. The bleak loneliness she felt was numbing her soul.

The unseen barrier still stood solidly between them. Their love had not been able to surmount it.

She shivered. Rand sat up and pulled the sheet over her, then he got out of bed to shake the blanket out atop her. He went to turn out the light. She welcomed the darkness. She heard his footsteps fading and bolted upright in sudden panic.

What was he doing? Was he preparing to leave? Her blood ricocheted through her veins until the crash of her pulse drummed in her ears. She sat in tense fear, waiting for him to say he was leaving her. Her fear increased with each of his returning steps.

A plump, slick weight landed on her lap. She clutched the satin of her pillow as he climbed back into bed beside her. She peered at him, unable to see anything in the darkness but his nebulous silhouette. The outline of his arm was barely discernible as he reached for her.

He pulled her into his embrace, sliding them both downward on the motion. "Sweet dreams," he said.

The steady thud of his heart comforted her as his fervent kisses had been unable to do. She snuggled into the soothing intimacy of his hold. "Thank you," she whispered tremulously.

"Go to sleep."

Clinging to him—and to the hope that the separation

between them existed only in her mind—she obeyed his command.

She woke to a feeling of emptiness. Without looking, she knew he was already out of bed. She missed the warmth of having him beside her. The bed seemed far too wide. . . .

The void was filled with memories of last night. Her heart thumped painfully in her chest as she lay listening to the faint buzz of his razor, the splash of water. She stared at the shadows crisscrossing the white ceiling and envisioned Rand's movements, the way he'd tilt his head as he shaved, the way he'd shift his weight as he washed. The picture was vividly real. She squeezed her eyes tightly shut and still she saw him.

Yesterday she had thought that if only they came together, if only they'd end the night by wrapping each other in a cocoon of love, then all would be well between them.

Last night she'd discovered just how wrong she could be. She recalled how, not so very long ago, she'd smugly thought that the bed was one place where everything was always right between them. Now she knew there was no sanctuary from this ever widening fissure that was rupturing their marriage.

The hope that it all existed only in her mind couldn't survive in the bright light of day. The truth would not go away. The dilemma existed, all too solidly real.

Both were ambitious, motivated to strive for the top of their profession; both had trained and worked hard to succeed in news broadcasting. It was natural that both should want the anchor position and want it badly. But only one could be hired. No matter how much they wished otherwise, such a deeply felt rivalry had to tax their relationship. The stress of the last weeks had proved that.

And it wasn't merely the competition that estranged them. The real problem, the one that pierced to the core of her being, lay in the outcome.

Fear raced in frozen tracks over her skin. She loved Rand, but she was afraid her love for him couldn't erase the hurt she'd feel if he were the one hired. She honestly didn't know if she could handle it. She wondered, too, what his reaction would be if she were hired, and didn't think he'd accept any more easily than she being bested by the one he loved. Sadness touched her. What was going to happen to them?

When Rand left the bathroom, she rose and headed directly for the shower. After she'd washed, dried, and doused herself with jasmine-scented powder, she slipped into a sunbeam-bright poplin shirtwaist she hoped would lighten her spirits. If ever she'd needed a boost in morale, this was the time. She examined her reflection, decided the dress didn't boost a thing, and expelled a gloomy sigh as she went into the kitchen.

Rand leaned against the counter, the pale slate-gray of his suit emphasizing his muscled length. It was her favorite suit and for no rational reason, seeing him in it added to her growing sense of foreboding.

"Not a very cheery day," he said, giving her a handful of vitamins and a small glass of juice.

She obediently swallowed and looked out the window. Imposing clouds clumped together, a low, gray ceiling that dampened the day and stole the rainbow from her sun catchers. The dreary sky seemed fitting to her mood. "Looks like we're in for storms."

"Sure does."

The constraint in his tone caught her attention. She slowly turned her gaze from the window to his face. It came as a shock to realize he was holding himself back from her. Although she'd wondered if he'd felt the same distance between them that she felt, she hadn't actually expected that he did; to discover that he must knocked the air from her lungs.

She gripped her coffee cup with icy hands and watched the steam waft upward. At least ten sentences stumbled together in her mind, ways to tell him how much she loved him, how much she ached inside over this conflict between them, how desperately she longed to ease his pain. What she said was "It's still not right, is it?"

"No."

"I'd thought, I'd hoped, last night . . ." She stammered into an awkward silence.

He stared into his cup, then flicked his gaze over her. "So did I."

"I love you, Rand." She felt it was hopelessly inadequate, but didn't know what else to say.

"You know I love you too," he said, then paused. She saw the unhappiness cross his face and felt her stomach clamp. "But love doesn't solve everything. We're going to have to work out a resolution if we're to keep from breaking apart."

The heat of the coffee burned its way down her throat. She didn't feel it. His words had numbed her. To hear her fear spoken aloud gave it a reality she didn't wish to face. *Breaking apart, breaking apart.* It hammered in her ears. She set her cup down and said faintly, "I don't see what we can do. There's no solution until the station makes its choice."

And maybe not even then, taunted her ringing ears.

Rand shifted restlessly, looking away from her. "I know we agreed not to let it disturb us, but I, for one, didn't realize the enormity of the strain this would have on our relationship. You have to admit, Nicole, the pressure has been terrible."

He glanced at her. She nodded. Dread crept into her veins. She didn't want to know, but she had to ask. "What are you trying to say?"

"I think one of us has to withdraw."

Every muscle she possessed tightened. Her entire body seemed rigid, unbending, unfeeling. "By one of us, I take it you refer to me?"

Did that stiff, haughty voice belong to her? It sounded alien, completely unknown to her.

"You'd be the logical one—"

"Logical? Why? Because I'm the wife, the little woman who should support her husband's career?"

"That's not a half-bad reason for starters," he snapped. "It'd be nice to have you actually on my side for a change."

He was a stranger to her. She didn't know this man who looked at her with such set animosity. Striving for a reasonable tone, she said as levelly as she could, "That's not fair, Randell, and you know it."

"It's not fair because you'd rather compete with me than keep our marriage together."

Her heart pounded so fiercely, she didn't know if she'd be able to speak for the pulse beating in her throat. She forced a gust of air out of her lungs and demanded, "What have you been doing, listening to Dee and the rest of the family spout their traditional role-playing garbage?"

"Some claim there's gold to be found in garbage."

"What's that supposed to mean?"

"Maybe you should try listening to them once in a while. Maybe you should think about being a *wife.* If you did, you'd pull your application."

"How can you ask that of me?" she cried, striking the counter with her balled fist. "What about my career? You've always said you wanted me to reach for the peak, but when it comes down to it, it appears you'd far rather be the King of the Mountain. It appears my career doesn't mean a damn thing compared to yours."

"Dammit, Nicole, I've put more years into this business, I deserve the chance."

"I deserve the chance too. Just because I haven't got your experience—"

"I'm telling you," he cut in sharply, "if you love me, withdraw."

She gaped openmouthed at his stony face. She couldn't believe what she'd just heard. The clamoring of her heart must have distorted her hearing. "Is that a command?" she asked heatedly.

"I loved you enough to give up a promising position just to be with you," he said in reply. "But you won't do the same for me. That tells me a hell of a lot about your love for me."

She didn't think she'd have to worry about her pounding heart anymore. It had ceased to operate.

"If you will recall," she said with deadly calm, "I never asked you to make that grand sacrifice. In fact, I tried to talk you out of it. Had I known you intended to throw it up at me in the future, I'd never have let you ruin yourself on my behalf. Maybe we should have spared ourselves all this and split up then."

With a forceful little jerk, he sloshed the remainder of his coffee down the sink and plunked the cup on the counter. "Maybe we should have," he agreed curtly, and headed for the door.

By the time she'd thrust herself into following him, he'd already slammed out of the apartment. She ran to the front window in time to see his motorcycle flying out of the parking lot. She watched until she could no longer see his black helmet in the distance, then pressed her forehead against the pane and miserably wondered what she had done.

The hope that Rand would have calmed down on his ride to the station was dashed the instant she arrived there. She walked into their office and he immediately walked out. It remained that way throughout the morning. On those occasions when he had to suffer her presence, he didn't so much as glance at her. Through her, but not at her. The pain of it was unexpectedly sharp. She hadn't thought anything could hurt more than the angry words that had passed between them earlier, but she discovered his silence hurt even more.

The worst part was not knowing how to deal with it. They'd had their share of disagreements in the years of their marriage, but nothing like this. Rand had lost his temper—rarely, but it had happened—but never, not once, had he been angry like this. He wasn't the sort to carry an argument on and on. Or at least, he'd never been the sort. Apparently he'd changed.

Circumstances changed and people changed with them. Part of the secret to a successful marriage was to adapt to each other's changes. Up to now this hadn't posed a problem for Nicole. She and Rand had changed, it was true, but they'd done so together, sharing more interests with each passing year. For the first time, change was pushing them apart, and it frightened her.

She didn't have time to mull over it. They were doing a live remote from the South County Center mall and she had to get going. She couldn't think of anything worse than having to spend the day putting on her public face with Randell. Not when she all she wanted was to sit alone in a darkened room and cry her eyes dry. But, as they said, the show must go on.

Driving to the mall alone in the sedan, Nicole swayed between a still-smoldering anger, a bitterly biting pain, and a nasty worry that he would never forgive her. Not, the anger in her instantly corrected, that she needed to be forgiven. He was the one in the wrong, asking—no, *demanding*—that she withdraw her application. The pain in her stabbed anew, renewing her worry, and the vicious mental cycle continued.

The station's vans were already parked near the entrance closest to the location of their shooting. An antenna disk rose like a beanie propeller from the top of one panel truck, while thick cables slithered out of the side of the other, winding into the mall. She acknowledged the engineers' greeting with a wave as she passed by.

Inside, on the center of three levels, a small set had been assembled. Their wicker chairs and coffee table were grouped together beside a square oak planter lush with greenery. A small bandstand stood to one side where the guest ragtime band would play later in the show. Eight floodlights on tripods surrounded the "set," and two color television sets were placed at angles to it. Barry and Ted relaxed near their cameras while Sharla went over the technical schedule attached to her clipboard. A widening circle of people clustered in the background while a growing throng of spectators pressed against the railing on the level above.

Nicole's eyes scanned all this within a fraction of a minute. Rand was nowhere to be seen.

She plopped into her wicker chair and pulled a small mirror and case from her purse. She daubed makeup on to remove the shine from her cheeks, nose, and chin and to hide the purplish crescents beneath her eyes. It was a darker base than regular street makeup, but even so, her face remained pale. She frowned at her reflection, then closed the case with a fierce little click that echoed her feelings precisely. Jamming it back into her purse along with the mirror, she shoved the bag beneath the coffee table.

Stunning bouquets of flowers bedecked both the center of the table and the space in front of it, adding a festive touch of color. She absently fingered the golden petal of a yellow mum and intently searched the sea of traffic flowing in and out of stores, up and down escalators, in all directions of the mall. Though she didn't see him, she didn't panic. Rand would turn up in time. He was too professional to let his private life interfere with his job.

Even as she thought this, she heard a sighing among the women gathered to watch the program and knew he was coming. She occupied herself with looking over the pink and yellow script sheets left on the table. He took his place in his chair. The slate of his jacket sleeve, his pantleg, dominated her peripheral vision. She ached to tell him she loved him.

"You'd better clip on your mike," he said as he attached his own to his blue-striped tie.

"I know my job, thank you," she instantly bit back. It

wasn't what she'd wanted to say at all, but it was too late. Already they were embroiled in another argument.

"Then do it," he was saying, and she felt compelled to snap "When I'm ready to, I will."

A young woman standing beside a baby stroller asked if she could take a photo of them. Rand's head jerked up. He looked to Sharla, who held up two fingers, then glanced at Nicole. She nodded. "Sure," he told the woman, who was already aiming a pocket camera in their direction. They both smiled, which Nicole privately thought absurdly ironic. The woman took two more shots, then thanked them, adding that they were a lovely couple.

"That's what you think," said Rand beneath his breath.

Nicole heard it, and though she'd thought the same herself, it stabbed her. She fastened her microphone on to her yellow dress with fingers that shook. When Sharla told them to stand by, she straightened in her chair and decided it was time to show him a thing or two. As the floor director extended her palm to signal Rand to begin, Nicole said brightly, "Good afternoon and welcome to *STL Noon.*" Camera two was on her immediately and she accordingly followed the red light to smile into it. "I'm Nicole Clarke. I'm here with Randell Clarke at the South County Center mall today with a wonderful crowd—"

Sharla gestured to the audience and they clapped, none of them aware of the unexpected maneuvering by the woman who smiled sweetly at her husband as she said, "And we expect to have a terrific time with members of the St. Louis Ragtimers, who'll be here to tell us about the upcoming National Ragtime and Traditional Jazz Festival." She stopped. Rand picked up the slack, saying, "Also today on *STL,* we'll take a look at some interesting day-trips you can take within the metropolitan area. Right now let's take a look at the news."

They alternated the news, giving each item from twenty seconds to about a minute, before they cut away to a commercial. As the miracle of electronics switched from the live broadcast to the taped commercial, Rand hissed at Nicole, "What the hell did you think you were doing?"

"Introducing the program," she explained, her prim look fully evident on her face. She fought to suppress twinges of guilt at her admittedly irresponsible move.

He smiled to the crowd in general and said to her in a low aside, "I was supposed to make the introduction—"

"Don't think I haven't noticed that you've always made the intros," she interrupted, waving and nodding at the audience. Her smile felt cemented in place, a rigid fixture on her face.

"So you take over without a word of warning. By God, I could wring your neck for—"

"Pardon me for pointing this out to you two," said Sharla, pushing aside the mouthpiece on her headset as she stepped up to the set, "but according to my schedule, Rand was on camera one for the intro. What gives?"

"Sorry, Shar," jumped in Rand before Nicole could even open her mouth. "I meant to change the schedule."

The floor director swiped her slender hands on her blue jeans, then readjusted her headset, mussing her short mop of hair and disguising the sarcastic twist to her mouth. "If you've got any other little surprises in store for me, do me a favor and forget 'em."

"No more surprises," he promised.

"Good," she said, and turned back to her position between the cameramen.

"You didn't have to protect me," snipped Nicole, feeling unreasonably certain he'd done so just to rile her further.

"I wasn't protecting you. If anything I was protecting the professionalism of the show. Of all the childish, amateurish— Welcome back to *STL Noon.*" His resonant, well-modulated voice replaced the harshly grating tone he'd used on her. "We're broadcasting from South County Center mall today . . ."

He gave the sports rundown; she reported the weather statistics. He introduced the author of a guide to day-trips in and around St. Louis, and Nicole interviewed the woman with practiced ease. "Thank you so much for joining us," she finished. "We'll be right back live at the mall after this."

On that cue Sharla again generated applause from the surrounding crowd. While the televisions showed the in-mall audience that home viewers were seeing a dog food commercial, Rand leaned slightly to the side and quietly stated to Nicole, "A childish, unprofessional, and asinine trick, my dear."

She smiled, nodded at him, and helped their guest unhook her microphone. The author left, and Nicole discarded the used script sheets. "Shabby is the word that comes to mind to describe your behavior," she said, still smiling. "Not to mention underhanded and deceitful. Besides which— Welcome to *STL Noon* . . ."

After her lead-in, Rand interviewed the spokesman for the Ragtimers about the festival. Nicole watched him and gave in to a flood of regret. She shouldn't have pulled that trick; he was right, it had been unprofessional. Her fury over his treatment of her didn't excuse it. She'd started the show off badly. The whole day had started off badly. She wished she could go back and start all over again. She wished she could erase their argument in the kitchen.

And as she wished, she vividly recalled Rand's deadly "if you love me, withdraw." Her anger rushed back in full force.

"When we return, we'll hear a bit of ragtime," said Rand. He discarded his script beneath the table and as he relaxed in his chair, she clipped out, "Where do you get off, anyway, telling me what to do? I'm not a dog. I don't obey commands."

He threw her a startled look, and she realized he had no idea that she'd reverted to their original argument. She knew she was being unreasonable, but she couldn't seem to stop it. She wanted to be unreasonable. Where was it written, she mentally demanded, that she had to be reasonable all the time?

"I do not intend, under any circumstances, to withdraw my application. You'd better accept that," she expanded.

A shuttered mask covered the startled look on his face. "What you do is up to you," he said coolly. He shifted slightly in his chair, just enough to turn his shoulder toward her without seeming to.

They came back on the air, and after a brief introduction the band began to play, blasting a cheery Dixieland tune throughout the mall. Nicole leaned back in her chair and focused on the banjo player in an effort to ignore the presence of the man beside her. It was futile, of course. Her mind was taken up with thoughts of him.

He loved her, he said, yet he had issued a demand that sounded ominously like an ultimatum. It was so unfair, so unlike Rand, she had no idea how to deal with it. Frank had said it was amazing how ambition distorted a person. He was right. Since the anchor opportunity had come up,

Rand had been like another man. Or perhaps he'd always been like this and she was only now seeing the real Randell.

A memory bolted out of the blue. Leaves scurrying briskly in a frosted fall wind that had lashed her hair into tangled disarray and stung red into her cheeks. She'd buried her face into the comfort of Rand's shoulder, leaned on his strength as the minister had laid her grandmother to rest. She saw Randell folding her into his arms, wiping away her tears and remaining understandingly quiet. He had known no words would compensate; he'd known she'd need his strength and support. She'd thought then that life without him would be unbearable.

That was the real Randell. And life without him would be unbearable. She loved Rand. He said he loved her. So what was happening to all that love?

The last of her anger dissipated, leaving only the pain and sadness. She was sorry they'd somehow felt the need to hurt each other. And the hurt cut deeper with each wound. They couldn't go on lashing out at each other and expect to resolve their problems. If she had to swallow her tongue to do it, she vowed not to spur this argument any further along.

Through the rest of the program, she refrained from any personal comments and wasn't surprised when he did the same. As soon as they signed off, however, she tapped his shoulder. He looked at her warily. "Do you need a ride back to the station?" she asked, working hard to make her query sound as inviting as possible.

His finely arched brows drew briefly down, then he glanced toward where Ted and Barry were switching off floodlights and folding the tripods. "No, thanks, I'll ride back with the crew."

While most of the audience wandered off toward other diversions in the mall, a few people hung around, inching closer. Nicole decided this wasn't the time nor the place to try to settle anything. "Okay, then, I'll see you there later."

"I may not get back to the station today," he said.

"Oh. At home, then. Shall I plan a dinner or not?"

"Not."

"Okay." She unclasped the mike from the neckline of her dress and stood. She didn't look at Rand, knowing that to do so would make it harder for her to leave without creating a scene. It took all her willpower not to reveal how much she was aching.

"Bye, guys," she said cheerfully to the crew, and walked out of the mall.

CHAPTER SEVEN

Long before she heard the throbbing rumble of Rand's motorcycle that evening, Nicole had realized patching up their argument wasn't going to solve anything. There was, as he had so brutally pointed out that morning, only one real solution. One of them had to give up the chance to become KSTL's newest anchor.

She had weighed everything and nearly concluded that she would do it. Given the competition—and Rand notwithstanding, there were some heavyweight contenders vying for that position—she didn't really believe she had a chance anyway. And though she wouldn't normally give a fingersnap for Frank's opinions, he'd said it had been Craig who'd told him women weren't really in the running. Craig was in a position to know. She'd thought briefly of asking him before leaving the station that evening, but the one opportunity she'd had, Craig had been swamped in work, so she'd let it pass.

She wished now she had interrupted Craig to ask that

question. Not that his answer would change things now. She held in her hand a crumpled letter that had tumbled the troubled kaleidoscope of her indecision into a set pattern.

She stretched out her hand and lifted the drape back to look out the window. Rand turned into the carport, got off his motorcycle, removed his helmet. Letting the drape drift back into place, she turned her gaze to the wrinkled paper. She smoothed it out and reread it.

The management of KSTL TV-7 would like her to submit an air check by the end of the following week. She was one of eight still being considered to replace Craig McCall. A final decision would be made once the audition tapes had been viewed. The signature of Josef Korsinski slashed across the bottom.

Hearing approaching footsteps, Nicole slipped from the sofa and walked toward the door. She paused by the end table to pick up a letter from atop the pile of mail she'd heaped there. As she listened to the scrape of Rand's key in the lock, she read his neatly typed name on the envelope. The door swung open, she held out her hand.

"Here, it's for you."

He frowned slightly and took the envelope from her hand as he kicked the door shut behind him. He glanced down at it, then up sharply at her after he'd seen the KSTL logo with its call letters entwined with a rendering of the Arch on the return address. "Did you . . . ?"

"Yes," she answered, and waved the crinkled letter. She watched him as he opened and read his letter. His hair was matted down from wearing the motorcycle helmet. She somehow resisted the urge to fluff it up with her fingertips. He finished the letter, refolded it, and replaced it within the envelope. "Congratulations," she said.

He slapped the envelope against his palm. "You too."

"I'm sorry about this afternoon, Rand. You were right. I acted childishly and unprofessionally and—"

"Forget about it. I didn't behave much better."

"But I was really at fault, jumping in at the lead like that." She nervously rubbed her hand down her thigh. She could feel her strained muscles through the lightweight white cotton slacks; like her nerves, they felt stretched to their utmost limits. If he didn't start acting like himself soon, she was afraid they'd simply snap in two.

"I said forget it. It's over and done with."

"We can't just forget what's been happening between us."

Lifting a hand, Rand rubbed his eyes. Lines of exhaustion tracked his brow and set grimly beside his mouth. When he lowered his hand, her heart turned over at the leaden way in which he looked at her.

"No, we can't forget it," he agreed. "But I'm not up to sorting out our problems just this instant. It's been a rough day and I'd like to relax a little, take a shower."

"Of course," she said instantly. "You go ahead. We've got all night to talk."

An odd expression crossed his features, one almost of denial, but she decided it must have been a trick of the dim lighting. When he went to shower and change she called their favorite pizza place and ordered a large pepperoni topped with all the extras. Then she settled into a corner of the sofa to wait. She drew her knees up to her chest and propped her chin atop them. The string strap of her tangerine camisole top slid down her arm, but she didn't notice it. She was too wrapped up in her reflections. What should she do? she wondered for the thousandth time. As far as withdrawing her application went, that had been decided for her when she'd received the letter. It was the problem of how to defrost Rand that had her heavy brows drawn together in frowning concentration.

She deliberately smoothed her frown away as he reentered the living room. She placed a smile on her face and kept it there. "I know you said not to plan dinner, but I got hungry so I called out for pizza. It should be here pretty soon."

He came to stand before her. A mingling of clean scents clung to him: soap, shampoo, freshly laundered shirt and jeans. She inhaled the nearness of him, then tilted her head back to look up at him. His hair was damply dark, the amber highlights hidden in the shadows. In contrast his face seemed somberly pale. His mouth appeared thinner and scarcely moved as he spoke.

"I suppose you're going to submit an air check."

Heart knocking, she swallowed back the impulse to match his contentious tone. "Yes, of course," she answered with outward calm.

"Of course," he echoed, but he was acridly bitter. "So where does that leave us? At a Mexican standoff?"

"I guess so. Until KSTL decides otherwise."

"I can't believe you'd let the station dictate the fate of our relationship."

She uncoiled from the sofa and came to her feet in front of him. "It's not the station, Rand. We've already made our decision. We made it the day we applied. And now we have to accept that neither of us is going to back down on it. I certainly don't expect you to, why should you expect it of me?"

He stared a long moment, then turned away. "I don't expect it of you. It's the last thing I'd expect of you."

She touched his arm. He jerked, but looked back at her. "Is it what you'd want of me, Rand? Really?"

The doorbell buzzed loudly. They stood, a frozen tableau, until the buzzer repeated. Then, muttering a soft oath, Rand crossed to the door and opened it. "Your pizza's here," he announced tonelessly, and she knew there'd be nothing settled between them tonight.

Nicole took the flat cardboard box from the fresh-faced delivery boy who gawked wide-eyed at her. "Say, aren't you the lady that's on TV?" he queried.

She nodded. "Yes, I am. Let me set this down and I'll get your money. How much is it?"

As she walked toward the dining table, Rand edged out the door. "I'll be back later."

She half turned. "Rand?"

"See you," he said, and vanished.

Short of dropping pepperoni pizza onto the living room carpet and pushing the delivery boy down the stairs, she couldn't stop him. She stood with a boxful of pizza warming her forearms, her face reflecting her frustration.

The youth mistook her look and said, "That'll be ten fifty-three, ma'am. That was the dude that's on the TV with you, right?"

"Right," she said, putting on a good show of will. The show lasted until the door clicked shut behind the pizza boy. In that instant Nicole stomped to the kitchen and dumped the pizza into the trash. Then she returned to the sofa to wait.

And wait. Each hour passed more slowly and still he didn't return.

At ten, watching Craig McCall's polished newscast, she visualized herself sitting there while Rand viewed her with envy and thought it'd serve him right. At eleven, she pictured with relish the bodily harm she'd inflict upon him when he finally dared to show his face. By midnight, she was torn apart by visions of his mangled body in a dark ditch and paced the tiny living room in nervous anxiety until she felt she could have crossed the country on foot and been less weary. Where was he? Was he hurt? Dead? Spending the night with someone else?

Despite the late hour, she called several of their friends, making apologies and inquiries in the same frantic breath. None had seen him. Her fears mounted. He hadn't called, he hadn't returned, he must be dead.

Her hand was on the phone, punching out the number of the police, when the door rattled. She raced to it, threw back the lock, and flung it wide. Her stunned surprise nearly matched his as he stumbled in. She fell back; he righted himself. They stared at one another.

"You opened the door," he stated in glassy-eyed accusation.

"Where have you been?" she demanded.

"I'm sorry, sweetheart, I didn't mean to be so late." He swung an arm around her shoulder and attempted to press a kiss on her mouth.

She inhaled a lungful of boozy breath, averted her head, and received a smacking kiss on her jawbone. Anxiety turned to anger. "Do you realize what I've gone through? I've been worrying myself sick, wondering where you were —"

"I was at Kelly's," he explained. He seemed to feel this should satisfy her and tried again to give her a kiss.

Jerking out of his clasp, Nicole backed away from him. He swayed ever so slightly and blew her a kiss. She gaped in disbelief. It wasn't that she hadn't ever seen her husband tipsy, it was the shock of seeing him tipsy *now.* She couldn't believe that he'd go off in the middle of an argument, leave her stewing for hours on end, to drink. It infuriated her.

She set her hands on her hips, planted her feet apart, and frowned fiercely at him. "You don't have to tell me you were at a bar. I can see that with my own eyes. Even if I couldn't see it, I could smell it from fifty feet. Believe me, Anheuser-Busch has nothing on your breath."

"You're exaggerating again, honey. I don't smell like a brewery. A pub, maybe, but not a brewery."

"I don't find that amusing, Randell. Do you have any idea what I've been going through? I've been worried sick."

He tried a placating smile. It didn't placate.

"The least you could have done was call," she pointed out coldly.

"I'm sorry—"

"So you keep saying," she interrupted. Her arms slashed through the air as she launched into her grievances. "But being sorry doesn't make up for the night I've spent. You sneak out in the middle of our argument, not telling me where you're going, leave me to worry for hours, then waltz—no, make that *stumble* in here and expect me to be appeased with a simple 'I'm sorry.' Well, *I'm* sorry, Rand, but I am not mollified."

"Coley—"

She didn't stay to listen. She whirled on her heel and charged down the hallway. She paused at the linen closet to dump a pile of sheets and blankets on the floor. Dramatically pointing a finger at them, she declared that he could sleep with them tonight, but not with her. Then she sailed into her bedroom and shut the door with a mighty crack that reverberated throughout the small apartment.

She expected, of course, that Rand would step over the pile of linens and come after her. Or at least that after he sobered somewhat, he'd join her in bed. But she suffered the torment of hours that crawled by like plague-infested decades as she waited for him and he did not come.

Finally, unable to sleep, oppressed by the loneliness of the bed and the misery of their continuing rift, she got up. The green digitals on the clock told her it was just after three. She slipped quietly into the living room.

Rand lay stretched out on the sofa, sound asleep. He hadn't made up the bed, but had cocooned himself in the blanket she'd tossed at him. She nobly disregarded the temptation to yank it off him and stomped back to the bedroom, slamming the door with a crash she fervently hoped, but sincerely doubted, disturbed him.

So once again they'd let a night pass with an unsettled argument standing between them. And for the first time, her husband had slept on the sofa.

The smoke unfurled behind him like a banner. Nicole waved it aside impatiently and caught up with the news director at the edge of the newsroom. "Lionel, please. What I have to say won't take long. I just need a few seconds of your time," she said, stepping aside to allow three obviously in-a-rush colleagues to dash by.

He halted and swept a wearily disgusted gaze over her. The lines in his forehead deepened. "If it's about the audition, that was just a formality, fair play and all that. Of course, we know how you look on-camera, but—"

"It's not about the air check," she cut in impatiently. "It's the PBS auction."

Disgust disappeared as wariness stole into his eyes. "What about it?" he asked in his most leonine growl.

"I can't do it," she said directly.

"Can't? What the hell do you mean, can't?" His cigarette bounced at the corner of his mouth; gray puffs billowed in her face. "Of course you can. You are."

"But, Lionel—"

He'd already sped on toward his office. Gritting her teeth, Nicole steamed after him, leaping out of the way as one of the assistant producers brushed past her. The assistant got to him first; by the time she reached Lionel, he was in the midst of one of his infamous rages. He snapped a memo in the air and glowered at the newsroom in general.

"Will you look at this? We charter a special flight to get that film and they *lost* it! Lost it! Without footage, that tornado isn't worth two minutes. Not one!" He ground out an obscenity, then commanded, "Cut the spot and fill it with the chemical plant walkout."

The assignment editor was changing the schedule as Lionel huffed. Nicole slipped around the editor to stand at the director's elbow. She waited patiently for him to exhaust the worst of his rage. When his balding skull turned from fuschia to its more natural pink, she pushed in front of him.

"Lionel, please, you know I wouldn't ask if it weren't important."

Swinging around, he gaped at her as if he'd never set eyes on her before in his life. Then disgust, redoubled, returned. "I haven't got time for—"

"Melanie could do it," said Nicole, naming the reporter who filled in for her whenever she was unable to do *STL*.

Lionel ran a hand over his few wisps of hair. He studied

her through narrowed eyes and she squirmed slightly, feeling he was seeing a great deal more than she wished him to. She hated having to ask this of him, but after last night, she had no choice. She had to do what she could to get out of doing that auction.

Abruptly he dropped his hand and shook his head, shattering her fragile hopes. "There's no way we can make a switch at this late date, you know that. You and Rand have been committed to the auction for months. Ads have been run promoting the two of you as a team."

"There's still two weeks, ads could be run announcing the change—"

He looked at her as if she'd just spoken in tongues. "Give me a break," he pleaded. "Who's gonna pay for it? You? Forget it, you can't back out now. Look at it from my viewpoint. It's just too damn late."

"But, Lionel—"

"No," he said, and turned to the producer with a finality that told her further pleas would be useless.

She left the newsroom in a state of dejection. She didn't know if she could face the upcoming ordeal. Each year, KSTL aided the local public channel's fundraiser auction by donating airtime, ad time, and hosts for the twenty-four-hour event. This year she and Rand had been given the hosting duty, for which they would not be paid and for which they'd exhaust themselves from five P.M. Saturday to five P.M. Sunday. When first told to do it, they'd groaned, but secretly had been happy to agree. It was the sort of insane fun they enjoyed. But Nicole knew there'd be no enjoyment now. How could she enjoy being constantly next to Randell, knowing he could barely tolerate her presence? If he wouldn't even sleep with her, he surely wouldn't want to work twenty-four continuous hours with her.

He wasn't at his desk, but she hadn't expected him to be. He was avoiding her, as he'd done ever since he'd gotten up this morning. He had apologized for not calling, for staying out so late, and she'd quietly accepted it, hoping that now they'd be able to talk things out. But he'd left immediately, once again taking his motorcycle to work. That was when she'd realized he didn't intend to ever talk it out with her.

Nicole had always been the sort to go after what she wanted, but this confounded her. She wanted to resolve things with Rand, but she wasn't willing to go as far as pulling her application to do it. They were at an impasse, one that last night had only served to aggravate further.

Not wanting to think about last night, she busied herself with writing the sports copy, then the weather data for the day's program. When she finished, she laid it on Rand's desk where he could add it to his script and complete the technical schedule. Then she escaped to the commissary.

This was not a room conducive to reflection. Fluorescent lights buzzed continually. Cakes of dirt clouded what view there was through the single window. Vending machines and pay phones were grouped together on one apple-green wall; a sink, a short counter, and a microwave covered another. Torn magazines and chipped ashtrays were scattered over round plastic tables. The atmosphere suited Nicole's mood perfectly.

She pumped a few coins into a machine and received a small cup of muddy coffee in return. Wrinkling her nose in distaste, she was about to occupy the nearest orange plastic chair when she heard her name called.

In the far corner Barry tilted back in his chair, rocking

it on two legs. He gestured for her to join him. She did so and his chair came down with a heavy thump. "Sharla said you wanted to talk to me."

Had it only been this morning? It seemed another lifetime since she'd spoken to Sharla. Her heart definitely wasn't in it, but she managed a smile. "Yes. I wondered if you had some free time this afternoon. I need to tape an audition."

"Sure thing. Unless the Arch topples over or some other catastrophe dictates otherwise, I'm free all day. You just let me know when."

"Thanks, Barry, I appreciate it."

"Hey, no problem." He looked her over closely, then rocked back in his chair again. His long, thin hair swayed about his shoulders. "So you made the cut for McCall's job, huh?"

She shrugged it off. "Umm. I think about one would be best. If that time's okay with you."

"For you, sweetheart, I'll make time."

It was a pretty lousy Bogart imitation, but it brought a genuine smile to her lips. "Thanks, really. It shouldn't take long, about ten minutes. I'm going to redo the *STL* newscast, but embellished."

"So what's Rand got planned?" he asked, and she choked on her coffee. She shook her head, muttered that she didn't know. He settled his chair on its feet. "Hey, are you guys still thinkin' about movin' to a new place?"

She aimlessly stirred her coffee with a white plastic stick. "I don't know. Maybe."

Privately she thought that at the rate they were going she and Rand would be looking for *two* new places. . . .

"If you do, you ought to consider the West End," he said.

He stabbed the tabletop with a long, thin finger. She absurdly noticed how disproportionately large his knuckles were and wondered why she hadn't noticed before. She realized he was still speaking and tried to pay attention.

"It's turning into one of the best neighborhoods, with old houses being refabbed and real professionals moving in."

"Thanks for the tip."

"Hey, no problem. The thing is, Sandy and I just moved in there and we think it's a great place to live."

She asked him about his bride and he grinned widely. He carried the rest of the conversation until they went into the studio just before airtime. He extolled his wife's virtues in a continuous monologue that had the effect of depressing Nicole beyond reason. She remembered when people had told her how Rand talked about her that way. Now he wouldn't even talk *to* her, much less about her.

She felt a perverse satisfaction that he'd have to suffer speaking to her during the show. But it was a double-edged sword, striking her just as sharply. She had to suffer being so close to him, behaving normally.

During the program, he seemed so like the old Rand that at times Nicole found herself amazed at his ability to act so convincingly. He smiled with seeming sincerity when he complimented her on her tailored turquoise dress, sounding just as if it were the first time he'd set eyes on it, when in fact he'd bought it for her himself at Neiman-Marcus. She didn't realize that she seemed just as sincere when she accepted the remark with a loving smile and a gracious "Thank you." It was part of their training, their professional expertise, to maintain the facade of a truly happy couple.

She didn't linger when the lights dimmed at the end of the show, but unclipped her microphone and left immediately. Rand didn't smile at her then, oh, no. His smiles were strictly reserved for the camera. When the red light was off, so were his smiles. Wouldn't the viewers be surprised, she thought with a gloomy sense of humor. If only the audience could see how they ignored each other during the commercials. Or better still, how they ignored each other at home. . . .

It was an effort, but she forced herself to shake free of her morose mood. It wasn't the humor to be in when taping her air check. She spent the next half hour rewriting several of the news items she'd covered at noon. At one she met with Barry at the news set and handed him a technical schedule of the items, citing which ones had videotapes, with the length of each noted to the second. Then she did a ten-minute "newscast."

"How was I?" she asked when she finished.

Barry stepped from behind his camera to hold up a thumb. "A ratings hit if ever I saw one."

A long, relieved sigh issued from her lips. She felt better than she had all day, all week. She thanked him, then thanked him again as he told her he'd leave the tape on her desk. His "Hey, no problem" followed her off the set. A wistful smile played at the edges of her mouth. Sandy Bosco was one lucky woman.

A shadow moved around the corner of the set's plywood backdrop. Nicole jerked to a stop. Rand stepped into the light.

"That tape will knock their socks off. You did a terrific job, Nicole."

For a moment she was speechless. Seeing him there had been a great shock. Knowing he'd watched her do her tape disturbed her, put her at a disadvantage. She wasn't certain whether to be pleased with his compliment or piqued at his secretive spying. "The tape still has to be edited," she finally said, a shade defensively.

"It'll turn out great."

"Thank you."

"No need to thank me for observing a fact." He shoved his hands into the pockets of his tan slacks, rumpling his sport coat in the process. He fixed his gaze intently on his shoes. "Nicole, I'm sorry."

"I—it—it's okay," she stuttered.

"It's not okay. I've hurt you. I haven't wanted to, but that still doesn't excuse it."

"I understand."

He looked up suddenly, his eyes sharply on her. "Do you?"

Her heart constricted painfully. "It's like you said. This—competing like this—it's a real strain."

"It's worse than that."

Yanking his hands from his pockets, he turned away from her. She wanted to reach out to him, yet she felt unable to do so. His stiff stance separated them. He was clearly unapproachable.

She wanted to cry out, "Don't! Don't turn away from me, don't divide us like this." But her vocal cords no longer seemed capable of producing that much sound. Instead she tentatively prompted, "Rand?"

He faced her. His expression was remote. "I've never been one to like being second best at anything. You know that. You know I strive to win. I don't like losing. But I could accept it if I lost out on the anchor job."

He spoke in a detached way that made her think he was merely mouthing words someone else was speaking. She hated it, she almost hated him for it. "So?" she said.

"It's not easy for me to admit it," he said, "but it's the thought of losing out to you that's sticking in my throat."

She drew in her breath. It whistled in her chest. "How can you say that?"

A rueful smile twisted his lips. "For all my liberated views, it appears I've a touch of male chauvinism. On some level, I need to be superior to my wife."

It was her turn to study the floor. Dirt filled the cracks in the wood. Wires leaped out in unexpected places, ready to trip the unwary. Her vision blurred until she saw nothing but the pain of this moment.

"In many ways," he was saying, "I've thought of you as my protégée. I was proud of you, but part of that pride was in my accomplishment. I found you, I helped mold you. When I realized my protégée actually wanted to challenge me on my level, it was like getting kicked in the gut."

"You've always said you wanted me to aim for the top."

"I always thought I meant it. But I guess you hit the nail on the head when you said I had to be King of the Mountain. I'm ashamed to admit it, but I just can't adjust to this rivalry between us." He stopped abruptly.

Such tension radiated from him, Nicole thought she could reach out and grab hold of it. She began to quiver. Was this what they were meant to come to? Was this the destiny for the two who had promised to love and honor and respect each other with such sincerity six years ago? She clenched her hands in an effort to still the trembling of her body.

"I can't back out, Rand, not even for you." Her whisper was a wavery strand of sound.

"I know. That's one of the things I love most about you."

Her eyes flew up to meet his. A sad, lopsided curve touched his mouth, and her heart constricted.

"You asked me last night if I wanted you to back out, remember? Watching you do that tape today," he said softly, "I wanted to sweep you into my arms and shout out my pride and love."

Great relief, sadness, and fear welled together in her soul. Relief that he still loved her, sadness that he still held himself so stiffly away from her, and fear for their future.

"But at the same time," he added, "at the same time, I resented you, Nicole. It was unfair of me to expect you to be the one to pull out—but I can't help feeling resentful that you didn't."

"But why? Why would you expect that of me? Rand, this isn't like you. . . ." Her voice dwindled into nothingness. There was nothing else she could say to the stranger looking at her with such detachment, saying such heart-shattering things.

"For one thing, I thought—apparently mistakenly—that you wouldn't want it as much as I." He stopped, expelled a gust of air that harshly resembled a laugh. "But mostly, Nicole, I just wanted you to support me, not oppose me. I've tried to deal with the fact that the job means more to you than I do, but—"

"That's not fair!" she burst out. "Am I accusing you of wanting the job more than me?"

"I know, I know." He sighed. "But we're not talking about fairness, we're talking about feelings. You accused me of not acting like myself. Well, I haven't felt like myself either. I've felt eaten up with anger and resentment."

The fear overrode everything else. She stepped forward, grasping his arm. He flinched and she fell back. Heartbeats counted out the passage of time while they stood transfixed, gazing at each other with love and pain and increasing loneliness.

"I'm sorry," he said. "I honestly don't mean to hurt you."

"You are hurting me," she whispered through barely parted lips.

"I know," he admitted sadly. "And I'm hurting too. We seem to do nothing but hurt each other lately. That's why I think I ought to move out for a while—"

"No!"

"Just until we can come to grips with this, Nicole. Or until I can. We're together so constantly—all day, all night—a separation will give us both time to think, to work this out."

"Don't do this, Randell. Don't do this to us."

He reached out a finger and gently traced the high ridge of her cheekbone with the tip. "I'm doing it *for* us, can't you see that?"

"No, no, I can't," she said. "Separation won't solve anything. We should work it out together."

"It's only temporary," he said, evading her statement. "We'll still see each other every day. But time alone is bound to do each of us some good."

She didn't agree, not at all, but she ceased opposing him. If it had been another woman, she'd have known what to do, how to fight back. But she didn't doubt Rand's love or his fidelity. That was what made her heartache so overpoweringly painful. How could she fight back when she herself, her ambitions and his, were the problem? The inextricable knot of their predicament was strangling her, but from some hidden source she found the strength to produce a wavery smile. "A man's gotta do what a man's gotta do, I guess."

Flashes of relief and love and hurt mingled over his face. "I love you. Don't forget that."

She nodded. She wanted him to hurry up and go. The tears wouldn't be banked much longer. He leaned forward, brushed his lips across the top of her hair. A tear spilled and another and then he was gone.

CHAPTER EIGHT

The lingering spring chill of early June was finally chased away by the onset of a hot, muggy Missouri summer. Thunderstorms and tornadoes whipped over the state, leaving a humid July in their wake. Despite her frequent wish to be struck by lightning or swept away by a funnel, Nicole remained disgustingly whole and unharmed. Except, of course, for her heart.

Her heart had been mangled beyond repair as days crept into a week and then into another and still Randell didn't come home. That first weekend without him she'd told herself she'd get through it with no problem. She'd lived apart from him before, she could do it again. But she'd forgotten what it was like. She'd forgotten how cooking for one was a chore, not a pleasure; how unenjoyable watching TV alone could be; how depressing it was to wake up in the morning with no one there to wish a good morning. She'd forgotten how achingly empty life could be. . . .

She doodled pointless spirals over the corner of a script page and thought about how tired she was. She hadn't realized how debilitating loneliness could be. The apartment that had always seemed so small was now large enough for her to feel lost in; at night she wandered restlessly from room to room to room, as if unconsciously searching for the man who was not there. When too exhausted to pace anymore, she collapsed onto a bed too cold and empty to permit sleep. While everyone else waxed golden with summer tans, she waned ashen with a sleepless pallor.

She thought how easy it would be if, like the more delicate women of another age, she could have taken to her bed. But she wasn't allowed such an escape. She had to live and work and act just as if her whole world hadn't shattered around her. In the beginning she'd told herself it would soon be over. Now she told herself she'd get used to it.

The steady clack of Rand's typewriter drummed in her ears. She cast a sidelong look across the aisle. As she watched, he paused to tilt his head back and drink from a can of cola. The muscles in his neck rippled. The blood in her veins thrummed and she knew she'd never get used to it.

He glanced over, caught her before she could avert her gaze. "You done with your script?" he asked with polite affability.

She wordlessly gathered the few pages together and, scrupulously avoiding his touch, stretched across the aisle to hand them to him.

"Great," he said as he took them. He quickly scanned the pages. His eyes narrowed slightly. She wished she'd erased the random scribbles at the top corner. They revealed too much. She hadn't been the sort of person to waste time in frivolous doodling and she didn't want him to draw any conclusions from her sudden indulgence in such idleness. But of course he made no remark about it.

They took extreme care not to make any remarks beyond the courteous byplay necessary between co-workers. Once, in desperation, she'd cornered him as the lights dimmed and the set darkened to ask him when—if—he intended to come home. He slid his gaze away from her. His face seemed utterly blank. Her nerves screamed into the waiting silence.

"Don't press me," he finally said, and something in her died.

"I wouldn't dream," she stated on an incisive bite, "of pressing you."

She pivoted and started to walk off the deserted set. He grasped her arm. She shriveled him with a look and he dropped his hand. "I love you, Nicole. You know that."

"Do I? You have a funny way of showing it."

He winced. "It's got nothing to do with how I feel about you. But with the way we keep hurting each other, I feel I have to stay away. Can't you see that?"

"No. I can't," she said, her voice harsh with pain.

"Nicole—" His hands came up as if to embrace her, but halted in midair as she stumbled blindly back, tripping over a thick cable in her haste to avoid that heartbreaking contact. She righted herself and they stared at each other across an arm's length. "Nicole, please listen—" he began again, but she turned and raced out of the studio before he could stop her. She couldn't take the agony of it.

A few days later, in a fit of rejected pique, she'd flung the technical copy at him, snapping, "Here. You do it. You do everything else."

He looked up at her in astonishment. "What's this?"

"You hog all the feature copy, you might as well have that too. And this," she flared, dumping an appointment book in his lap. "Try some of this busywork you've left me and see how you like it." For her parting shot, she fired, "I've been blind all these years to just what an MCP you really are."

He followed her stormy exit from the office. "If you want to talk about how blind you've been," he fumed under his breath, "don't forget how conveniently you've failed to see how selfish you've been."

A host of withering retorts came instantly to mind, but she didn't utter any of them. The vivid hurt marking his face stopped her tongue. She did an abrupt about-face. He trailed her back to her desk, this time apologizing. Not daring to speak, fearing she'd inflict more hurt on them both, she'd accepted his explanation that he hadn't meant it with a curt nod and went back to work.

The next morning, the feature news tapes were left on her desk, with a note asking her to please edit them and write the copy. But after that they'd scarcely spoken except for two days ago when he'd commented that she looked pale and she'd angrily snarled, "What do you care?" before taking refuge in the ladies' room. Since then they'd retreated to cool civility.

She pulled out a round stand-up mirror and began applying her program makeup. She daubed it on slowly, pretending to herself it was to insure the thorough elimination of her pallor. Through the angle of the glass she observed Rand as he hauled the last sheet from his machine and began counting lines of script to figure the time of each item. His hair looked longer, nearly covering his ears and scraping the collar of his off-white shirt. Hadn't he remembered his appointment with the hairdresser? Actually, it looked good at that length. She imagined the soft feel of it upon her fingers as she rubbed his nape. . . .

As she hastily pitched the makeup and mirror into her desk drawer, Sharla appeared and demanded to know if the technical schedule were ready yet.

"Almost. Give me five minutes," said Rand.

"Cutting it close today," Sharla noted, a tinge of anxiety clear in her tone.

"We'll make it," he assured her, adding a confident smile to convince her.

Nicole looked away, hating him for smiling at Sharla that way, hating Sharla for inspiring the sort of smiles she no longer received from him. Abruptly she pushed back her chair and left.

She avoided him until airtime, then headed for home as soon as they'd wrapped the program. She was supposed to get well rested before the start of tomorrow's telethon auction. Not that she expected to be well rested. She never rested well anymore. The most she hoped for was to doze fitfully and wake relieved to have made it through another night. She was even tempted to take a sleeping aid, something she'd normally not have considered for a moment. But nothing was normal anymore.

She hadn't even had the energy to again attempt persuading Lionel to drop her from the auction. She'd thought briefly about going over his head to the producer or general manager, but she didn't act upon it. That would have taken more verve than she possessed these days. So, though she dreaded doing it, Nicole was going to have spend the weekend with the husband who no longer wanted her.

* * *

The woman in the mirror looked stunning. Nicole felt rather silly. It was absurd to be wearing a full-length formal dress in midafternoon. She was going to look a fool when she drove to the studio. But still, that woman in the mirror was gorgeous.

The gown accounted for most of the effect. Its tight-to-the-skin sleek bodice and dramatically flaring full ruffled skirt evoked the sophisticated romanticism of Hollywood's Golden Age. The lapis blue deepened the blue of her eyes so that for once, Nicole actually thought they were quite pretty. The dusky strands that casually cascaded from the stylish topknot of her hair contrasted with the creamy white skin of her exposed shoulders. Though she normally didn't wear much jewelry, for this occasion she was swimming in sparkles. On the one slim shoulder strap she'd pinned a winking diamond rosette, while a V-shaped tiered necklace circled her neck, and matching earrings dangled from her ears. Of course, they were all paste, but she knew that on the set they'd flash as brightly as the most scintillating diamond, and that was all that mattered. The business was, after all, one of perceptions.

Perceptions. She rubbed her hand over her bared shoulder and thought about the images the business projected. The home viewer didn't realize how distorted the reality could be. The "steel" file cabinets on the news set that were actually painted plywood; the paned "window" in the *STL* set that was really masking tape checkered over clear plastic; the happy, loving couple whose marriage was falling apart.

Diamonds danced and ruffles swished as she spun away from the mirror. Such thoughts weren't productive, particularly now, when she had to present the image, not the reality.

She slid into her strapless black heels, drew a deep breath of courage, and left. She sincerely hoped Randell remembered their conversation about Fred Astaire and Ginger Rogers; if he hadn't, she'd kill him. They'd only talked about it once, the night they'd been assigned the auction duty, lying in bed and laughing over how amusing it would be to dress up for the occasion. She'd suggested Groucho and Harpo, but Rand had said, no, he wasn't spending twenty-four hours hunching over a cigar while she honked a horn at him. "So who would you like to be?" she'd asked.

"Fred Astaire," he promptly said. "Sophisticated, dashing, dancing Fred Astaire. I've always wanted to be a sophisticated man with a sophisticated woman in my arms."

"You," she said as she snuggled more closely to him, "just want to be a man with a woman in your arms, period."

"That too. But you'd make a terrific Ginger Rogers."

"With my hair? Ginger never had hair this dark."

"She should've," he murmured as he nuzzled his lips within the black tangles. "Ol' Fred doesn't know what he missed. . . ."

His mouth had wandered from her hair to her ear to her neck and that had been the end of the conversation. But on the wild hope that he remembered it—and to show him that she had—she'd dressed the part. She thought she was probably making a fool of herself, opening herself up for a great hurt, but she had to risk it. The unspoken message would say what her heart clamored to say, but she could not.

Her pulse was battering wildly when she entered the public-channel studio. It was ridiculous, she'd just seen Rand yesterday, but her blood didn't seem to respond to rationality. It continued to careen unsteadily in her veins as she followed the youthful auction volunteer to the manager's office. She focused on the red, white, and blue band of the girl's straw hat and tried to calm her shaky nerves.

The girl paused, pointed to a door, and said, "That's it. Your husband's already there. Just go on in."

"Thank you," said Nicole, hoping it hadn't sounded as squeaky as she'd thought it had. She inhaled deeply and entered.

He hadn't forgotten. He wore a white tie and tails that would have done ol' Fred proud. She stared, mesmerized by the debonair gentleman standing before her. Was it really Rand? Had he grown? Lost weight? He looked taller, slimmer, more elegant than her Randell.

"Thank God," he said, and the indented smile was definitely her Randell's. "I was terrified you'd have forgotten and I'd be stuck here in this monkey suit."

He'd spoken to her, really spoken to her. He hadn't sounded as if he were speaking from a distant Arctic ice cap; he'd sounded warm and familiar. Her sudden burst of happiness expressed itself in a pert laugh. "And I was shaking all the way here with fear that you'd forget and I'd be the one stuck looking like this."

"Me? Are you kidding? Forget my chance to be Fred Astaire? You know it's not like me to forget a lifelong ambition."

The word hung a moment, suspended between them. She stared at the sensually full lips that had spoken it and felt such an aching she wondered how she kept from crying out.

He broke away from the tension and plucked a shiny top hat from the office desk behind him. Setting it at a jaunty angle atop his head, he shuffled a soft-shoe across the width of the office. Whirling around, he waltzed back to the desk. He flashed her another of his endearing smiles. "So? How'd I look?"

The aching was sweeter now, bittersweet. "You look . . . dashing," she said softly.

"What about dapper?" he asked, leaning on an imaginary cane. "Fred always looked dapper."

"Fred never looked so dapper."

"You're ladling it on too thick, my dear. I can't hope to out-dapper Fred. Fred never had a crooked bow tie." He stretched his neck and tugged on the small bow. "I don't know how he did it. Can you get this damn thing straight?"

She walked to him with a rustling swoosh that echoed in her ears. She pushed his hands away from his bow tie and began reknotting it. He smelled of starch and soap and lime. Her own jasmine perfume wafted up to mingle with his scents.

"That's a spectacular dress," remarked Rand.

"Thank you."

"If Ginger had worn a dress like that, Fred would never have danced with anyone else."

Her hand shook; she had to redo the knot. She didn't know how they'd come to be exchanging flirtatious quips, but it was heady, intoxicating—and dangerous. If Rand realized the effect he was having on her, it would leave her vulnerable, open to more heartache. Determined to keep it light, she tossed back, "Now who's ladling it on? Ginger had closets and closets full of dresses like these."

"But she never looked like you do in that one."

She managed to set the bow straight and step back. The glow in his eyes made her breath catch in her throat. "Wait'll you see the bill," she laughed shakily, "then you'll think twice about this dress."

The words were chased by the thought, *If you ever see the bill,* and the electric thrill she'd been feeling since walking into the room died. This was nothing more than playacting, projecting the image of the clothes. The reality was the lonely bed in the lonely room at home.

"Nothing could change my mind about that dress. Or about how you look in it," he murmured, no longer sounding frivolous.

As if to ward him off, her hand came up. "Don't. Don't play with me, Randell. I can't bear it."

"I'm not playing." He stepped forward. She stepped back. "I've missed you."

His simple sincerity halted her retreat. She dared to hope that what she saw was real. The guarded mask he'd worn for so many weeks was gone. What she saw on his face was a reflection of her own loving and aching and needing.

He took another step, reaching for her. She stood, waiting for him. The door flew open.

"Things are about ready to begin," announced a deep voice.

They spun around. A silver-haired man with wire-rimmed glasses beamed at them. "You look marvelous. Quite an addition to our auction."

Laurence Keller was the general manager of the channel and, like all station managers, was more of a money manager than a people manager, but his greeting was cordial. After shaking hands and exchanging pleasantries, he explained their schedule for the next day.

"Ten-minute breaks every hour, of course, and in the early morning hours when viewership is down, each of you can spell the other for a couple of hours to catnap. We have a storeroom with a cot set aside for your use, and a local deli is donating sandwiches throughout the auction."

Keller ushered them out, and Nicole followed him in relief. She was grateful for his interruption. She'd had time to realize what a colossal mistake she'd been about to make. She had been about to fling herself into Rand's arms and that wouldn't have resolved anything. They needed to talk. She needed to know whether he'd worked out his inner conflict, whether he was ready to accept the rivalry between them—to accept her.

The studio was a cacophony of activity. Three large boards were set up to list items for sale and the current bid on each. Another rotating board listed special items, things like box seats at a Cardinals' game or dinner and entertainment aboard the *Goldenrod* showboat. Two rows of tables with telephones stood ready for volunteers to accept the bids. Around all of this scurried people with banded straw hats, carrying merchandise to display tables, pencils and pads to telephones, coffee to co-workers. Camerapeople adjusted equipment, auctioneers read over lists. Everyone seemed to be talking at the same time.

"Three minutes!" the director shouted and the frenzy increased. Workers positioned themselves at the phones. Crewmen straightened headsets and talent settled on their marks. Nicole and Rand stood at the center of the set, facing the cameras.

"I have missed you," he whispered to her while nodding

at a local radio celebrity who was one of the first auctioneers.

"I've missed you too," she said out of the corner of her mouth, "but that doesn't change anything."

"One minute!"

The volume of discordant noise rose as everyone scrambled to be ready on time.

"The popcorn poppers are missing!" someone yelled. "Where the hell are the poppers?"

"Maybe not," Rand was muttering, "but at least—"

"You two are simply gorgeous," declared an auctioneer who was a popular anchor at a rival station.

"Thanks, Debi." Nicole swished her skirt with a flourish. "We thought we'd class up this act."

"It needs it," cracked the floor director. Amid the general laughter of those near enough to hear the byplay, Rand continued doggedly, "At least it's a start. I've wanted—"

"Fifteen seconds!" More panicked rushing. "The poppers are still missing!"

"Find them!"

"I've wanted to tell you, but you didn't—"

"Ten seconds!"

"You didn't seem to want to listen."

The director's palm went up and over. A red light glowed atop a camera. Rand smiled with easy charm. "Good evening. Welcome to the Annual All-night Auction . . ."

From that moment on, they had little opportunity to talk. Introducing the auctioneers who changed at regular intervals, plugging the need for funds to support the public channel, stressing the tax deductible overbids, and other such work occupied them. Even when they weren't directly on camera, they were immersed in the business of preparing for the next cue or dealing with continually erupting crises. The popcorn poppers were found and duly auctioned off, but it seemed each hour some other object was misplaced to send them all into a frantic search.

Nicole didn't really mind the constant bustling. It kept her mind from lingering in the quagmire of her marital problems. She didn't want to think about the elation that had rushed through her when Rand said he'd missed her. She didn't want to be misled into believing everything was going to be magically restored to happiness. It couldn't be. Not as long as the anchor job remained between them. So she threw herself into the auction and, for a time, shoved her personal problems out of her mind.

Before she left for her first break, however, she seized the opportunity to inform him soundly that it just so happened she'd always wanted to listen. He, on the other hand, hadn't wanted to talk. He hadn't, she finished on a gust of resentment, even wanted to *be* with her. She darted away without giving him a chance to respond and spent her ten minutes regretting having said it. What if she'd ruined the tenuous harmony they'd been sharing tonight?

As soon as she reappeared on the set, Rand instructed the crew to hum "Stardust" while he scooped Nicole into his arms and twirled her about the studio. Phones began ringing crazily. The crew hummed harder, they whirled in a hushed whoosh of ruffles. The band of his arms about her felt so good, so right, her heart threatened to explode with the joy of it. She wanted to tell him how much she loved the closeness of him, how much she loved him. But she seemed to have expanded her quota of courage with her earlier speech. The most she dared was to glance up at him.

He gazed down at her, his somber face softened by a tender smile. "Your dancing's improved," he said.

Relief that he apparently didn't hold her speech against her was quickly followed by surprise. This was not what she'd expected him to say, not by a long shot. She raised her brows questioningly. "I've always thought I danced rather well."

"Don't you remember that show we did on the river-boat?" he asked.

"Oh, Lord, don't remind me. I get seasick just thinking about it."

"Remember the way you tumbled into the band when you tried to dance—"

"For the thousandth time," she interrupted saucily, "I did not tumble. The boat pitched me over."

"Sure, Ginger, sure," he agreed, obviously teasing. He swung her to a stop right on center mark and began speaking smoothly to the camera.

The banter continued. Rand seemed determined to make her laugh, to make the evening shine for her. Nicole was afraid she'd wake and discover this was all a dream, that the glinting smiles she received were conjured out of her yearnings. But the hours passed and with each one her happiness increased.

Though she felt wired and ready to work the night through, Rand insisted she take a catnap. "You just don't realize how tired you really are," he said. "You've got circles under your eyes the size of half-dollars."

"Oh, those? Those have nothing to do with this. Those are permanent fixtures."

There was a pause. She could have yanked her tongue out for alluding to their estrangement. The flash of pain over his face had been unmistakable. But he let it pass.

"I'll permanently fix you, if you don't get going," he threatened as he turned her around and sent her off with a pat to her rear. She went without further argument because she didn't want to do anything to jeopardize their current accord. And because she really wouldn't mind being alone to think about all that had occurred this evening.

She lay down without the least expectation of sleep. The cot was surprisingly comfortable. She stretched and yawned and dreamed of Rand.

She woke feeling strange and disoriented. She tried to roll over on her side. Arms, warm and masculine, caught and held her, keeping her from falling off the narrow cot. Her gaze focused fuzzily on the hand, traveled up the arm and settled on Rand's tenderly crooked smile. This was the best dream yet. She let her eyelids drift back down.

"Oh, no, you don't," he said, gently propping her upright. "It's time for you to get up and dance for your supper, Ginger."

"Do you love me?" she asked drowsily.

"More than anything," he said. He abruptly released her, and the next thing she knew, a cup was warming her hands, steam was tingling her nose. She took a sip of coffee, looked at the walls of steel shelving lined with row after row of tapes and canisters, and came fully awake.

"What time is it?"

"Five."

"Five! That means I've been off for three hours. You should have wakened me an hour ago."

He shrugged. "I figured you needed the extra sleep."

She set down the cup and got up. "Well, it's your turn now."

"Actually, I'm not even tired. This thing's a snap. We're already halfway through and I feel as if I've just started."

"That's what I felt like and I went right to sleep." She shook wrinkles from her dress and tucked escaping strands back into her topknot. "How's my hair look?"

"Adorable."

"Rand, I'm serious."

"So am I. Everything about you is adorable."

An inner warmth spread outward, glowing within her, brightening her. "Sweet dreams," she said as she blew him a kiss and slipped out the door.

During the next three hours, she thought several times about the way in which Rand had answered her, telling her he loved her "more than anything." She wished she'd been more awake, for then she'd know whether or not she'd imagined the earnest fervor of his tone. Had he meant just what his words said or had she imbued them with what she wanted so badly to hear?

She didn't have an opportunity to ask him, for the pace of the auction picked up throughout the morning and afternoon until they were being pulled in all directions, feeling like puppets on short strings. At last the final bid was announced and the red camera lights went out. Standing in the rapidly emptying set, they took stock of each other. Exhaustion disappeared, replaced by a bubble of happiness Nicole couldn't contain.

Her happiness was centered, as it always had been, on Rand. His tie was now tilted askew, the starch in his collar had long since wilted, and the jaunty top hat had developed several interesting dents. She tried to stifle her giggle, but it rapidly escalated into a full-fledged laugh. "You look, you look," she gasped, "like a bedraggled penguin."

He drew himself up and stuck his chest out. "You've been drinking," he accused.

"F-F-Fred never looked like a p-p-penguin!"

"You're drunk," he said again, and she shook her head, helpless with laughter. "You're obviously in no condition to drive home. You must be drunk."

"Punch-drunk," she said, but privately thought she was intoxicated with love of him.

"Come on, I'm taking you home," he said. He tucked her into his hold and they rolled out into the bright summer evening locked arm-in-arm. After being inside for the past day, it somehow surprised her to see all that sunshine paving the lot. It added to her feeling of dreamlike unreality. She squinted into the sun, scanning the lot. "Where's your bike?" she asked.

"Don't worry about it. I'm taking you home."

She stepped out of his arm. She scrutinized his expression. It was carefully blank. "There's really no need. I was just being silly. I'm perfectly capable of driving myself home."

"I want to take you home," he said. He held out his hand to her. "I want to go home. Will you have me?"

The white gold of his ring mirrored the sun's rays. It was a warm and merry shine, rather like the glow they'd shared all night. She stared at it and wavered. They still hadn't really talked. But did it matter? Wasn't the important thing to be together, to be beside him, to have him next to her? Eyes still riveted on his glinting ring, she took his hand.

They ambled to the sedan. He drove and she dozed. Still groggy, she leaned into his shoulder as they climbed the stairs to their apartment. His hand rubbed over her arm, soothing and stirring all at once. Her body began to tingle in anticipation.

It seemed to take a year to fit the key in the lock, to turn it, to open the door. Inside, westering sunlight filtered through the drapes to bleach the darkness. Her eyes adjusted easily, dim objects quickly became clear. The sofa, the loveseat, the lamps on the tables. The hunger stamped on Rand's face.

Desire blossomed, full and ripe, within her. The taste of his lips, the touch of his hands, the texture of his body against hers—she remembered them all, yet memories could not satisfy her. She wanted Rand, all of him, all his love merging with hers.

She raised her hands to her hair. Pins scattered like windblown seeds to the carpet. Her hair spilled like spring rain to her shoulders. Her earrings capered brilliantly within the dark cascade. She dropped her hands to her nape, to the clasp of her necklace, but Rand shook his head, stilling her motion.

"Let me, Coley. Let me undress you . . . all of you."

Her gaze locked with his. Her body tensed. She feared her heart would pound right out of her chest. And slowly she lowered hands, which felt like deadweights, to her side.

Without removing his eyes from hers, he leisurely ran his hand up her bare arm, pausing at the shoulder. His fingers toyed with the brooch before slipping beneath the slender strap. He inched the strap downward, then bent and kissed her exposed shoulder. She quivered.

He placed a finger on her collarbone and lightly traced the line of the blue bodice with the tip. Snowflake kisses softly drifted in the path of his fingertip. She closed her eyes. She bit her lips to keep from begging him to hurry.

The pleasure was almost unbearable. It was sweet, slow, exquisite torture.

The heat of his body radiated into her blood as he moved closer, wreathing her with his arms. He skimmed over the slick material from her ribs round to her back. He dragged the zipper down its track with agonizing deliberation.

In a silken susurration, the dress slithered downward. His mouth followed its descent, gliding from collarbone to breast, humming against her skin. Her nipples tightened in response. He playfully flicked his tongue over one taut peak, and she could no longer bear the waiting.

"Rand, no more, please . . ."

"But I want more," he murmured, his breath moistly caressing her breast. "I want all of you."

"And I . . . want you . . ." she breathed huskily.

A lapis pool of ruffles rustled at her feet as she pushed him away and stepped from the confines of the dress. She kicked free of her heels and wiggled out of her hose. A triangle of rose silk floated to the floor, and she stretched out her arms to him.

He didn't hesitate a heartbeat. He lifted her up and carried her toward the bedroom. She unknotted the bow of his tie and loosened his top three shirt buttons. She slipped her hand inside, splaying her fingers over the firm, warm contours. The tip of her little finger brushed the tip of his nipple and she felt it harden. Beneath her palm, his heartbeat rapidly kicked. Her own vaulted dizzily. My God, she had missed him!

He lowered her onto the bed, then stepped back to strip off his clothes. As the rumpled pile on the floor grew, so did her excitement. In the meandering haze of light, his skin shone a muted gold. It seemed appropriate to her, for she treasured him.

He muttered a curse. She propped on an elbow. He was naked except for his opened shirt. A curve tilted her mouth upward as he thrust his arm at her. "These damn cuff links," he grumbled, "must have been designed by the sadist who invented the chastity belt."

"Not quite, darling," she laughed and proved her point with a teasing caress from his belly to his thigh.

His groan was nearly a growl. "Do that again," he commanded.

But she sat up and began unclasping the initialed links. "You haven't been fair, you know. You undressed me. You should have let me undress you."

The shirt rustled as it fell away from him. The bed sagged. He pressed her back into the mattress. "Do you really think," he asked as he lay atop her, "that we could've waited that long?"

Her laughter met his in a mingling of breath. Then laughter was drowned in a floodtide of passion. Their lips met in a kiss that was more than a kiss. It was a commitment.

They touched each other in exploration, with a sense of rediscovery. He stroked her hair, her cheeks, her shoulders, electrifying her nerves with the sensual friction. She rubbed her hands over his back, down his spine, around his hips, generating a quivering within herself as well as within him. He slid his hands over the fullness of her breasts. He watched as he massaged the grainy peaks to rigidity, then raised his eyes to her face.

"I feel as if I've waited years to taste of you again," he whispered. He lowered his mouth to the puckered crest.

She gripped him tightly, pulsing with desire. But she did

not hurry him. This time there would be no need for haste. This time, they would linger over their love.

They took the time to savor this renewal of their vows. He avoided her most sensitive places, seeking to rouse her slowly, inch by inch. She, in turn, drank in the wonder of him sip by sip.

Without him, her senses had been deadened. Now they came fully alive, and she reveled in the joy of sensation. She gloried in the hard flexing of his muscles, the musky scent of sweat on his skin, the moist softness of his lips on hers. Everywhere she touched, he felt warm and wonderful.

And everywhere he touched, she felt hot and sensual. He tracked kisses from her breast to her belly and she throbbed. He glided his palms down her rib cage and she quivered. He kissed and caressed and roused her to a trembling of white-hot need. When he at last he fused his being with hers, she rose up to meet him with an explosive exaltation.

Together! They were together as they were meant to be. Giving and taking and sharing the love they'd pledged to each other. The rightness of it heightened her pleasure to an unparalleled degree. Nicole truly thought she could burst from the fulmination of it.

The bed rocked. The room darkened. Their breathing labored over the drone of the air conditioner. The love between them magnified. Several times they spiraled toward fulfillment only to pause and prolong the exquisite pleasure. Tension rose beyond control and they were transported, their love transformed. Together, they floated in a nebula of celestial bliss.

Together . . .

CHAPTER NINE

His breathing gradually eased. Her heart slowly settled to a stable beat. Satisfaction spread languidly through her, reaching the farthest tip of each limb with equal repletion. But her feelings extended beyond the physical. Her spirit felt whole, complete, as it hadn't for weeks. She stirred beneath his weight and sighed with pleasure.

He mistook her action and raised himself away from her. The air stirred by the conditioner immediately breezed over her sweat-slicked skin, chilling her. She coiled her arms about his neck. "Stay on me."

"Wasn't I crushing you?"

"No. Even if you had been, I wouldn't care. I like it."

He repositioned himself beside her, then tangled his arms and legs about her. "How's this?"

"Heavenly. I've missed this—you—so much, so very much."

An echo of remembered pain breathed through her words. He tightened his hold and burrowed into her neck.

She clenched him to her, relishing the squeeze of his arms about her. It had been so long, too long. Never again, she silently vowed, never again would she let him walk out of her life. They were meant to be together.

The downy softness of his hair grazed her shoulder. He nuzzled along her throat, then up her chin. At the edge of her mouth, he paused and blew teasing little kisses over her lips. "If I ever," he said between breaths, "do anything half as stupid as leaving you again, I want you to have me committed."

"You missed me?"

"I thought I'd go crazy with missing you."

She laced her fingertips into his hair and played with the dark thickness of it. "You could've fooled me. I got the impression you could barely tolerate being around me at work."

He expelled a breath too harsh to be a laugh. "I couldn't. It was sheer torture for me to be with you each day, yet be without you each night."

"You didn't look tortured." The hurt in her lashed out. "Quite the opposite."

"Darling, I'm sorry," he whispered. "Is there any way I can make it up to you? Anything I can do to have you forgive me?"

The hurt eased. She kissed him softly. "I forgave you already, don't you know that?"

"I've hurt you so much—"

"It's over now," she soothed, hugging him to her breast. But within her heart she wondered, *Or is it?* The conflict over the anchor position still lay between them. . . .

His lips pressed over hers. She nibbled and tasted the sweetness of his kiss. "Yes, it's over now," he murmured, and her doubt spread like dandelions.

She didn't want to dig into that patch of distrust. This was the time to sow the seeds of reconciliation. Determined to ignore the doubts, she grasped the first thought that passed by. "What shall we do about your bike? Should we go get it tonight or wait until after work tomorrow?"

He raised his head. He looked somewhat sheepish. "Well, actually, it's already at the station, our station."

"You didn't ride it to the auction?"

"No. Doug Sims gave me a ride over there."

Two and two came together slowly. She saw his mouth tilt upward, his eyes gleam in the dark. She ran her hand over his hip and mused aloud, "You meant to drive me home all along."

"Yes."

"Why?"

"I thought I'd already explained. I missed you like hell. I needed to be home with you."

"Why?"

"Now that's a loaded question," he said on a wisp of laughter. Then he sobered. "I feel as if I've been run through an emotional wringer. I hurt like I never hurt before, and the worst of it was, I was bringing it on myself for resenting the very things I'd loved most about you—your independence, your competence, your refusal to strive for less than the best."

Her fingers doodled aimless patterns on his hips and back. The thrill she felt over knowing he'd planned to come home to her was dampened by the threat still hanging over them. Essentially nothing had changed. He'd come back, but those things he resented, those were still an integral part of her. For now, his love had overcome his resentment. What would happen tomorrow?

She fixed her gaze on her fingertip as she drew it up his rib cage in a series of careless circles. "None of that's changed. I don't understand what spurred you into coming home."

"This wasn't an impulse, Nicole." He propped up on an elbow and watched her fingers continue their design on his skin. "I've thought about us, about what was happening to us, until my head ached. The day you challenged my doing all the feature work, I was stunned into seeing that I'd been subconsciously holding you back for years. Once I began to look beyond my own hurt, I realized you were right. Separation's no solution to a problem. We have to work it out together."

"I told you so," she said primly, then carefully added, "but you still didn't come home."

"I really wasn't certain you'd have me. I thought you'd tell me to go to hell. You can't imagine how my heart jumped tonight when you walked in wearing that dress and I knew you'd remembered. I think I loved you more in that moment than I ever have before."

As her spiraling fingertip whirled higher, so did her spirits. "You think you love me, huh?" She laughed.

"There's nothing that matters to me as much as you do," he said simply, "as much as our relationship."

The circling stopped abruptly. She stared at her finger, motionless an inch away from his nipple. "Not even the job?" she asked, and didn't recognize that tremulous voice as her own.

"Not even the job."

She looked at him then. He was regarding her intently. She started to look away, but his hand came up to trap her chin in place. "Look at me, Nicole. Believe me. The job no longer matters. Only you matter, you with me."

"But what if—"

"It doesn't matter," he cut in firmly. "Being without you taught me that nothing else matters as much as being with you. I want to wake in the mornings with you. I want to laugh with you in the daylight and love with you in the moonlight. I just want to be with you. Nothing else matters."

"But—"

"Say it. Say nothing else matters," he ordered.

The mouth that had been so lovingly soft, so tenderly teasing, was now a thin, stern line. The fingers that had swept over her with such gentle passion now bit firmly into her jaw. She thought better of raising objections. "Nothing else matters," she said obediently.

But she didn't believe it.

His fingers loosened, his thumb delicately stroked her cheek. The harsh line melted from his lips as he bent and kissed her. And as her mouth opened to fully accept his kiss, she thought it wouldn't last, couldn't last. He thought he meant what he said, but if it came down to a test, would he feel the same? Would he still feel nothing else mattered if she was hired as anchor and not he? Would she be able to feel it didn't matter if he was hired?

Again she backed away from probing it too deeply. The scars had to heal. She nestled within the comfort of his embrace and desperately hoped he was right, that nothing else did matter.

"You know how much I missed you?" he asked abruptly. "I even missed seeing your hot curlers spread out over the sink in the bathroom."

She laughed softly. "And I missed seeing the tangled heap of your socks dumped in the closet."

"I missed the obnoxious way you chew ice cubes."

"I missed the dreadful way you dip onions into peanut butter."

"The crunch of those cubes—"

"The sight of those gooey onions—"

Suddenly they were laughing and kissing and loving all over again. And in the ecstasy of it, the demons of doubt were exorcised, if only temporarily.

"Are you crazy?" Eva eyed Nicole with the look of one contemplating calling for men with large butterfly nets.

Nicole hadn't even realized herself what was in her mind. If she had been asked point-blank, she was certain she'd have denied even considering withdrawing her application. Yet when Eva had mentioned that Joe's secretary thought there was going to be an announcement at the end of the week, she'd faced Eva and blurted, "I'm thinking of telling Lionel to cross me off the list of candidates."

Eva had reacted with all the disbelief Nicole herself felt. Her eyes had widened—two round purplish dots behind the tinted lenses. She'd shaken her head until her blond puff of hair lost some of its fluff. Her gaze swung between Nicole's reflection in the mirror and Nicole, as if unable to determine which was real, which the illusion.

"Are you crazy?" she repeated, her voice rising shrilly. "You can't back out now. Why on earth would you want to withdraw?"

That, of course, was the sixty-four-dollar question. Nicole leaned on the marbled vanity and intently studied the salmon swirls surrounding the sink. The ladies' room was not the place for a heart-to-heart, and Eva Baere wasn't the woman she'd select for a confidante, but a great desire to talk to somebody, anybody, overwhelmed her.

She licked her lips, sought a way to begin, and said, "It's not that I want to, precisely, but Rand and I have been having some trouble—"

"I thought you'd resolved that," broke in Eva, and immediately had the grace to look embarrassed. She evaded Nicole's eyes, averting her gaze to her own reflection. She plumped an already fat blue bow on her blouse and muttered, "Well, everyone knew you two were having some difficulty, but Doug said he thought you'd patched it up over the weekend."

"Does anyone around here ever talk about business or sports or the weather or anything but the latest rumor?" demanded Nicole in a furious huff. "Honestly, this place is little better than a henhouse where tongues continually cluck to no purpose."

"But I still don't understand why you'd have to withdraw," said Eva, getting back to the point with a reporter's tenacity. "Why not Rand?"

Nicole rolled her eyes. "Be serious."

"Look, Nicole, I can't counsel you on your marital problems, but I can tell you this. If I'd made the cut—"

"You applied?"

"If you could call it that. I asked Lionel what my chances would be and he laughed. I took that as a gentle hint to forget it. But the point is that if I'd made the cut, I'd feel obligated to run all the way with it."

"Obligated? That's a strong word. Why obligated?"

"KSTL needs a female anchor and you're the best chance we've got to become the first one. If you back out, you're not only sacrificing a big opportunity for your career, you're blowing it so far as other women are concerned."

She mulled on this. Eva's fiery defense of feminism

definitely made a point. There would be a real sense of accomplishment in being the first woman to break that particular sex barrier at KSTL. She couldn't deny that the success of it would taste sweet. But no matter how sweet, the flavor would be soured if it hurt her relationship with Rand. Would she really want such a bittersweet victory?

"I don't think I've got a serious chance of getting it anyway," she said.

"Maybe, maybe not. The thing is you can't just give up the chance." Eva caught Nicole's eye in the mirror and held it. "You'll probably tell me to mind my own business, but I've got to add this. I don't know what's been going on with you and Rand, but I do know this. He adores you. It's the kind of love that goes so deep it has no ending. Whatever you think this job is doing to you, his love is strong enough to bear it."

Nicole turned on the faucet and plunged her hands under the spray. "Yes, well, thanks for listening to me, Eva. I'll think about what you said, really I will."

After a wavering hesitation, Eva accepted this dismissal. Left alone, Nicole splashed the cool water over her face. It tingled and revived. She patted her face dry with a paper towel and deliberated over what to do. In her heart she knew Eva was right. Rand's love was strong enough to accept whatever happened. Last night he'd finally convinced her of that. He had folded her within his arms and loved her until she could no longer doubt him.

It was her love she doubted. Was her love strong enough to bear the outcome of this competition? Sadness flowed through her as she admitted her uncertainty about the answer. The only solution seemed to be for her to withdraw. Then she would not have to feel that she had somehow failed, that she had "lost out" to Randell. Nor would she have to suffer any self-reproach for somehow being selected over him. If she withdrew, there would be no resentment, no guilt.

She had told him she couldn't withdraw, even for him. That had been true. She couldn't back away from an opportunity because he told her to, because he resented it. But she could do it for herself, for the two of them. If, as Eva said, it would be a sacrifice, it'd be a sacrifice Nicole was willing to make. She was more than willing, she *wanted* to do it.

She saw it so clearly now it stunned her. When she'd blurted it out to Eva, it had been like test-driving a car to see how it would run. She'd tested the idea and discovered she liked it. The solution was there, as it had always been, only now she didn't resent having to take it. It was what she wanted.

She crumpled the paper towel between her fists, then jauntily tossed it into the wastebasket beneath the vanity. For the first time in nearly two months, she felt like the real Nicole Clarke. She left the ladies' room with her old decisive stride, exposing her legs the full length of the slit up the side of her white linen skirt. The cranberry sleeves of her blouse billowed as she moved. She was a woman who knew where she was going and why.

Lionel was in the midst of his usual attempt to tear the few ashen wires of hair from his head. She didn't wait for him to notice her. She slapped the flat of her hand on his desk and didn't bother to excuse herself for interrupting him. "I need a word with you, Lionel. Privately," she said in a voice of command.

He stubbed out his cigarette and leaned back in his chair. He folded his hands neatly over the front of his apricot shirt and leisurely assessed her from top to toe.

When he was done, he rested his gaze on her determined face. Finally, he growled, "What is it this time?"

She glanced around. Two producers were huddled together in the corner office, a correspondent had his feet propped on his desk as he talked on the phone. She decided not to press for any more privacy than this. Lionel had his limits, as she well knew. She stiffened her spine and stared at the "Murphy's Law" calendar pinned to the wall beyond his shoulder.

"I wish to be withdrawn from consideration as a replacement for Craig."

The thump of a cigarette pack brought her eyes down to his. He took his time over striking the match, lighting, and inhaling. He blew a perfect ring that drifted toward her, elongating and dissipating in the air. "Joe might not like this," he said.

"I'm sorry. I realize it's late, but even if you were to hire me, I couldn't accept."

"You couldn't, eh? Why not?"

"My reasons are personal. The point is I don't wish to waste any more of the management's time in considering me."

"Noble of you," he said with mild sarcasm. Several small rings puffed her way. "Well, far be it from me to push you into a job you wouldn't want. Not," he hastily added, "that I'm implying you would have been hired."

There was an odd sense of deflation, a feeling that there should be something more, that he should have tried to talk her out of it. It wouldn't have done him any good, of course, but still, he could have made the attempt. She tapped a fingernail against a black marble paperweight on his desk and waited. Smoke funneled as he whipped back to his desk and began shuffling papers from one mound to another.

"So," she said, "that's it? I'm out?"

"If that's what you want," he said.

"Yes, it's exactly what I want."

"Okay, then."

"And, Lionel?" He looked up, impatience pulling his shaggy brows downward. She said tensely, "I don't wish for anyone else to know about this."

"Yeah, sure, okay."

He'd already gone back to his paperwork. She turned and marched out of the newsroom. With each step, her spirits rose, elevated by a certainty that she'd made the right decision. Now she would be able to glow with a happy pride if he should get the position, her feelings wouldn't be stained with jealousy. If there was disappointment for herself, it was only fleeting. There would be other opportunities, opportunities that wouldn't mean competing against Rand. Her relationship with Rand meant more to her than anything, including her career. She didn't know why it had taken her so long to see this, but now that she had, she didn't intend to ever forget it again.

The anniversary she'd feared might not be celebrated at all was celebrated in style. Randell barbecued steaks on a small kettle grill on the balcony while she tossed greens in a creamy buttermilk dressing. A white tablecloth was spread on the living-room carpet and a champagne bottle was imbedded in a bucket of ice beside it. Corn on the cob and hot rolls completed the meal; roses and two brightly wrapped packages completed the decor.

Nicole leaned against Rand's chest and licked butter from her fingers. Rand fluffed the hair from her nape and watched. "I take it you enjoyed the meal," he said on a hint of a laugh.

"Mmm," she assented. With a last loud slurp on her index finger she added, "This has been much better than last year, don't you think? Really, I far preferred this to going out like we did then. Tony's may be one of the most famous restaurants in St. Louis, but Tony has nothing on you, Mr. Clarke."

He lifted her hand, inspecting her fingers. "I definitely agree. This has been better than last year." He dipped her index finger in his champagne. "Every year with you gets better." He licked the champagne from her finger and her heart fizzed with excitement. "Happy anniversary, Mrs. Clarke."

"Happy anniversary."

She dipped her finger again in the champagne, then traced the outline of his lip and kissed the bubbles away.

"Umm, the only way to kiss," he murmured.

"Oh, I don't know," she said saucily. "Offhand, I can think of at least a dozen other ways."

"Like how, for instance?" He looked down at her with an air of innocent interest.

"Well, there's the no-frills peck for starters," she explained in her best instructor's voice. She demonstrated with a brief buss that Rand gave a thumbs-down to.

"Definitely not," he complained, "in the same class as the champagne kiss."

"You didn't specify class. You said ways. Now shut up and let me count the ways." She raised to her knees, set her hands on his shoulders and eyed his mouth seriously. "Next there's the parted-lips-but-no-tongue-action, which is considered quite proper for first dates."

"This isn't a fir—"

She muffled his protest with an example, which immediately led to one of the parted-lips-with-tongue-action variety, which led to several other unnamed, uncounted ways. The remainder of the picnic was forgotten as they twined over the cloth. It was playfully carefree and heart-stoppingly wonderful. Nicole had never felt happier.

Any twinges of regret she'd felt for her lost career chance were dispelled by the bliss of being reunited with Rand. Although by some tacit agreement they'd avoided probing into their recent wound, over the past four days they'd talked as never before about their commitment to each other and their future together. Their pledge to make their marriage last held a new depth of meaning. That they didn't discuss the estrangement or the cause for it suited Nicole perfectly. She was more than willing to let the scars heal first. She knew if they talked about it at all, she wouldn't be able to hide the truth of what she'd done from Rand.

The ringing of the phone jarred them apart. Rand's elbow knocked into his glass and champagne splashed over the carpet. He cursed. She giggled and sprang up to answer the phone. "Leave it," he said, but she was already lifting the receiver.

While she spoke with her parents, Rand mopped up the spill. Then he got on the line to accept their good wishes, and she started clearing away the dishes. After he hung up, she spurned his suggestion to unplug the phone and pick up where they'd left off, somewhere around number eight.

"You know your folks will call, not to mention at least half your siblings," she said.

"Precisely why I want to unplug the phone," he explained. "If we keep getting interrupted, we'll keep losing count." He paused. He grinned. "On the other hand, let 'er ring."

"Sorry to disappoint you, darling," she said as she whipped the white cloth from the floor with a snap, "but I've got better things in mind."

"Better than counting the ways to kiss me?"

"Much," she assured him. She folded the cloth into a neat square, then sat cross-legged in front of the two packages. She poked a finger into the red ribbon on the larger one and declared, "I want to open my present. What is it?"

He slid lithely into place beside her. "Why don't you take the wrapping off and see? Although," he added on an injured note, "I can't understand how any package could hold more fascination for you than my kisses."

"Easy," she said dampeningly as she ripped into the red ribbon with enthusiasm. The bright yellow-and-red wrap came off in shreds. The brown box was embossed with the gold emblem of a famous store in the Plaza Frontenac. Nicole whistled soundlessly. "Hope you didn't break the bank," she remarked dryly.

"Oh, I left a little something in the account." He reached over her and lifted the lid off the box.

From amid an acre of tissue paper she drew out a stunningly simple day dress of lavender flowered with tiny forget-me-nots. It was the sort of clingy, casual dress that looked inexpensive and cost the earth. She jumped up to hold it against her and saw the flash of something fall from the skirt. She bent to retrieve it, but her hand faltered. "Oh, Rand." She sighed. "Oh, Rand."

He scooped the sun catcher off the carpet and held it out to her. "So you'll always know mine belongs to you," he said.

The heart-shaped glass seemed to be a deep maroon

upon her palm, but when she raised it to the light, it shone ruby red. She looked at him over the glass heart and blinked back tears. "Oh, Rand," she said again.

"There's an uncovered patch on the kitchen window," he said helpfully.

She took the hint and used the time it took her to hang the sun catcher on the window and her dress in the closet to regain her composure. She returned to the living room to find him vigorously shaking his package. "I do hope," she drawled, "you haven't broken it. I don't know if it can be replaced."

His hand stopped in mid-shake. He gently lowered the package to the floor and gingerly tested the ribbon. She sat down next to him and watched as he unwrapped it a patch at a time. And for the first time all evening, a small cloud dimmed her happiness. She wished she could tell him of the gift that had no wrapping. But that was the one gift she'd never be able to tell him about.

A jar of crunchy peanut butter emerged from the box. He cast her one quick, doubtful glance as he set it aside. Doubt became delight when he discovered the green onions. Affixed to the silver string neatly binding the bunch together was a tag that said simply, HAPPY SIXTH. Rand lifted his gaze. "I love you," he said.

Within the incandescence of his love, her momentary melancholy melted away. After all, the purpose of her sacrifice wasn't to glory in it; it was to enable her to glory in Rand's promotion. Which she fully intended to do. She was going to burst with pride when he became the new KSTL anchorman. She wouldn't let herself think of reacting any other way.

Today was the day everyone said Joe's announcement

would be made. Today was the day Rand would become the new anchorman. She dressed with special care, donning the new lavender dress with an amethyst choke necklace, and never let her mind linger over thoughts of what might have been.

"You always amaze me," said Rand as they drank their coffee within the cheery spray of sunlight through stained glass. "You manage to look absolutely adorable every day. And never more so than this morning."

"I could say the same of you," she said, and meant it. He wore her favorite gray suit, with a shirt of transluscent blue that she thought exactly matched the shade of her eyes, and a navy club tie her parents had given him the first year they were married. "You look as dashing as you did when you had on tails."

He set down his coffee and eyed her intently. "Are you trying to tell me," he finally asked, "that I look like a bedraggled penguin?"

They left for work on a note of intimate laughter. Nicole was more certain than ever that she'd done the right thing. Rand was more than her husband, her lover. He was her best friend and he was worth any sacrifice.

Expectation crackled in the air. Whispers soughed with it. Glances glittered with it. Bodies tensed with it. Yet the morning dragged on and nothing happened. Even Ginny at the front desk had no further news. When Nicole had met this morning's guest—a woman who'd won a contest to be completely made over by local beauty experts—she asked the receptionist what the word was. Ginny's round cheeks sagged and she shook her head. She had, she admitted sadly, no idea. Nicole thought she might start screaming if something didn't happen soon. Her nerves were stretched to the breaking point.

Even the technicians seemed to feel the mounting tension. Three distinct miscues marred the program that noon. Sharla added to the comedy of errors by running the TelePrompTer too quickly, causing Nicole to fluff more than one line. She noted that Rand was the one person who didn't seem fazed by the murmurs, the looks, the mistakes. Her pride in him bounced high.

Although they usually grabbed what lunch they could at their desks, they went out to a nearby deli with the crew and a gaggle of reporters to dawdle over hoagies and beer. When they returned to the station, Nicole stopped off at the ladies' room to freshen up while Rand went on into their office. Alone, she could no longer dodge the pangs of regret. They were tiny, it was true, but they were sharp nonetheless. Never knowing if she might have made it was what pricked the most.

She quickly finished brushing her hair and dropped the brush back into her purse. She dropped her regrets as well. She'd get over them. Other opportunities would come her way. Another Randell Clarke never could.

In their office, Rand was nowhere in sight. She glanced around. No one was in sight, but a white, typed sheet lay squarely centered on every desk. Josef Korsinski had announced the decision.

The memo was tersely to the point. When Craig McCall departed at the end of the week, weekend anchor Vincent Scapella would assume the weekday duties; Frank Walters would take over as weekend anchor.

Nicole read the memo through twice, then read it word-by-word again. She couldn't believe it. There must be some mistake. Vince was good, but he was no Randell Clarke. And as for Frank, why, that was laughable. At the end of the fourth reading, her disbelief turned to outrage.

How dare they not hire Rand! He was the best man for the job, and she would let them know it. She shot out of her cubicle and down the corridor.

Joe wasn't in his office. Or at least that's what his secretary insisted. Nicole was not about to be stymied. She wheeled and whisked straight to the newsroom. Clusters of two, three, and four people were dotted throughout, talk of the memo circulating noisily among them. She didn't pay them the least attention, but bore directly down upon Lionel's balding head.

Someone stood talking to the news director, but she didn't intend to let a little thing like that stop her. She sailed up to Lionel's desk, brushing past the other man without even looking at him.

She braked to a halt and hotly demanded, "What on earth can Joe be thinking—"

Even as she spoke, she heard, "Isn't it past time that a woman be given the chance—"

Her startled gaze flew up to Rand's face. His equally astonished one dropped down to hers. Lionel shoved both hands over his skull and actually grinned.

"Well, well, well, if it isn't Mrs. Clarke come to join this conference," he drawled. "Don't tell me. Let me guess. You've stormed in here to tell me that Rand should have gotten the anchor job."

"Yes," she admitted, wondering at the amusement that shone like a beacon in a fog on Lionel's smoke-hazed face. But given her cue, she charged ahead with her protest. "I can't believe you'd make such a stupid mistake! Rand's the most qualified newsman—"

"What I can't believe," broke in Rand with a fierce anger that took her by surprise, "is that they'd overlook *your* qualifications. This could warrant filing a sex discrimination suit. And you can tell Joe," he added, stabbing a finger at Lionel, "that I intend to back my wife to the hilt."

"There's no need to back me," she put in, but he paid no attention to her. Still waving that warning finger in the news director's face, he stormed, "Okay, so maybe Vince was a better choice for weeknight anchor, but to put Frank in over Nicole on weekends is absolutely ludicrous! She's far more qualified than he'll ever be—"

"*You* make Vince look like a student," she interrupted. "I can't see how anyone could think Vince a better choice than Rand, let alone Frank. Somebody's got some explaining to do, Lionel, and if Joe's going to hide in his office, then I guess it's up to you."

The crack of laughter that exploded from Lionel wiped the frown from her face. She gawked at him in stupefaction, then glanced at Rand. He was staring at Lionel, his face filled with a puzzlement to equal her own. They waited wordlessly for the director to regain his composure.

Still chortling, he at length straightened in his chair and eyed them both. "Your noble defense of each other is touching," he stated, "but misguided. Believe me, had it been possible to do so, Joe and I would have given serious consideration to your qualifications."

"And just why wasn't it possible?" demanded Nicole, her temper rocketing again. "What's wrong with Rand's qualifications?"

"Nothing, nothing at all," chuckled Lionel. He shook his head. "But as you'd both withdrawn your applications, there was little Joe or I could do."

"Withdrawn!" exclaimed Rand and Nicole in unison.

"Withdrawn," Lionel confirmed.

CHAPTER TEN

They gaped at each other in stunned disbelief.

"Why on earth would you—"

"How could you—"

"I suggest," said Lionel dryly, "that the two of you go somewhere else to thrash it out. As amusing as it's been, I can't waste any more time on you. Believe it or not, I do have work to do around here."

They walked out of the newsroom in silence. Following Rand in a daze, Nicole still tried to assimilate that he'd actually withdrawn his application. How could he? Didn't he realize opportunities like this didn't grow on trees?

He led her into the deserted studio, past the news desk neither of them would occupy, toward the darkened set of *STL Noon.* Their steps echoed into the stillness. The beige canvas that hung in a semicircle around the set glimmered eerily in the dimly lighted room. Cameras squatted on triangular bases, looking like ancient monoliths sculpted by a curious accident of nature. They sat in their accustomed chairs and Nicole felt a sense of disembodiment. She looked down upon the two of them and saw two silent silhouettes against an opaque backdrop. Reality had no bearing on the scene. Was this a dream from which she would soon waken?

"I don't understand it," Rand finally said. His resonant voice brought her back to reality. "Why did you withdraw?"

"Why did you?" she countered.

"I've already given you the answer to that," he said. A loving smile gleamed at her. "Nothing else matters to me as much as our relationship."

"Your career should matter. What you gave up . . ." She gestured toward the news set and her voice trailed sadly away.

"So did you," he pointed out. "Yet you'd told me you couldn't withdraw."

"I changed my mind."

"Why?"

The simple question encompassed a complexity that befuddled her. The impulse to say "Because it's a woman's prerogative" died unspoken. This was the time for them to come to a complete understanding, to clear the weeds tangling the path of their communication so they might not stumble in such a way again.

"Lionel said it was nobility, but I don't think it was that at all," she slowly began, then picked up steam. "It was fear. Fear of losing you again, permanently. Those two weeks without you were good in a way because I realized how much I needed you." Something between a sigh and a laugh issued unbidden from her. "I really do need you."

"And I need you."

The depth of his sincerity exhilarated her. "Works out

well that way, doesn't it?" She laughed and he joined her. Even before the last vestige of their laughter faded, she'd again turned solemn.

"I guess I never before realized," she mused, "just how much you must have done to keep our arguments from flaring into battles over the years. This time you were angry, really angry, and it scared me."

"I hadn't noticed you cowering," he said wryly.

"No, but that's because I was angry too. Even though I knew you were right when you said the only solution was for one of us to withdraw, that we weren't going to be able to deal with the rivalry between us any other way, I resisted it. Mostly, I think, because you'd sounded so me-master, you-slave when you demanded I be the one."

"You had every right to resent me for that, Coley."

"Oh, I did, believe me. I was shocked and hurt and furious."

The flowers in the set's centerpiece were wilting. Rand plucked a still-fresh white carnation from the center of the arrangement and handed it to her with a rueful smile. "A peace offering," he said.

Twirling the stem between her fingers, she inhaled the scent and absorbed the peace he'd offered. This was, she knew, yet another milestone in their relationship. One that did, indeed, bring her inner peace. She knew with unalterable certainty that they would never again come so close to breaking apart. They had gone through a raging fire and come out stronger, as strong as tempered steel. There would undoubtedly be other crises in the years to come, but whatever their future brought, she knew they would be able to face it together.

"You couldn't have been more shocked than I," he continued, "to discover that streak of chauvinism in me.

I'd always viewed myself as a totally liberated male. But suddenly I had to face up to the ugly fact that I didn't want my wife besting me. So added to all my other turbulent feelings, my resentment and anger and hurt, was a heavy dose of self-disgust."

"I still don't understand what made you decide to withdraw. I mean, you didn't have to fear *my* walking out."

The emphasis was a verbal slap, and he winced to receive it. "But I feared having you tell me not to come back," he said on a harsh note of pain. "I feared having already lost you."

She extended the carnation to him. "My turn. I promise not to throw that up in your face ever again."

He accepted both the flower and the promise. "And I promise you, Nicole—a solemn vow—never to walk out again. From now on, we resolve our problems together."

"I'll hold you to that."

"You won't have to. *I'll* hold me to that."

Her heart lifted, her spirit soared. "Let's say we just hold each other and let it go at that," she suggested pertly.

"You're on." He grinned. "Not for me the lonely nights on uncomfortable hotel beds. It was while I was lying awake in that dreary hotel for the umpteenth night in a row, wondering what the hell I was doing there when I should be home with you, wrapped in your arms, that I realized I'd do whatever I had to in order to come home to you. . . ."

"Took you long enough," she mumbled, and he waved the flower under her nose. She smiled sheepishly and took it.

"So anyway, I decided then and there to set things to rights between us. And that included going straight to Joe and telling him to scratch me out of the running."

"That was before the auction, wasn't it?"

"The day before," he confirmed.

She nodded. "I knew it. You were completely different that night—my old Rand back in full, delightful form."

"Your form wasn't so bad, either, Ginger."

Memory captivated them for a magic moment. Then the spell dissipated and Nicole sighed heavily. Regret, remorse, retrospection began to weigh down on her. All the "should haves" and "if onlys" rushed in. As her spirit sagged, the carnation drooped within her fingers. "It seems sad and stupid, now, doesn't it? I mean, we should have been able to deal with the notion of one of us getting ahead of the other. Instead, we both gave up a big opportunity. It's stupid."

"What we gained is worth far more," he said softly.

"But at what cost?" A burgeoning sense of loss and injustice grated her voice. She spread her hands outward, indicating the empty set in one agitated sweep. The plywood and plastic seemed to mock at her, at them. "At what cost, Rand? You're a reporter, a newsman. You shouldn't be stuck here, in this *living room,* chatting with beauty experts!"

"I thought you were satisfied with this."

Fearing to see the accusation so carefully absent from his tone, she couldn't meet his eye. Instead she steadily contemplated the puckering petals of the flower. "I was," she replied more quietly. "But I've been drop-kicked out of my complacency. I see now what we could be doing, should be doing. We had a chance for one of us to make it, and we threw it away. What a foolish, foolish waste."

Rand leaned over and cupped her hands in his. Twining his fingers with hers over the flower stem, he turned her other palm up. He lightly brushed his lips across the soft center in tribute. So gently did he ease the sorrow from her soul, she was scarcely aware of the transformation of her feelings. All she felt was the flutter of that gossamer kiss and her throb of response.

When he raised his gaze to meet hers, his eyes were dark, nearly black, with feeling. "No matter how unwise," he murmured, "I'd do it again, to keep from losing you."

"Oh, Rand!" She stopped, swallowed, and said huskily, "That's the most idiotic thing you've ever said."

"Umm, maybe." He knelt before her. "But you know, I read a poem once that said something like, 'kisses are a better fate than wisdom.' And considering all the ways you can kiss, my darling wife, I'd have to concur with that."

Emotion, raw and potent, threatened to gush forth in a torrent of joyful tears. She fought them off with a shaky laugh. "That might not be too wise either. You could be getting a raw deal. How do you know how many ways I can kiss? I never even finished counting, remember?"

"All the better to start counting now," he drawled suggestively.

Every cell of her being was imbued with a radiant love for him. "No need to rush," she whispered. "We have a whole lifetime to count them."

"Well, yes," he agreed, inching closer, "but it wouldn't hurt to get started on it. After all, we'll have some other business to keep us occupied in the future."

"Oh? Like what?" she asked, backing away from his kiss. She was teasing him now and enjoying every minute of it.

"Like making ratings history with *STL* in the October book," he said.

His thigh grazed her knee and his hands brushed

against her arms as he gripped the chair, pinning her into the seat. He pressed forward. She ducked. His mouth landed above her right temple.

"That still leaves plenty of time for future counting," she pointed out breathlessly.

"Yes, but in the meantime we'll be busy with convincing somebody to hire us"—he nuzzled from her temple to the edge of her lips—"as the first husband-and-wife news anchor team."

"And just who do you think would hire us? Two at a time is a mighty tall order. Anchor spots don't grow on trees, you know." She blew out a long, tempting sigh.

His breath merged with hers. "We'll go to Timbuktu if we have to. All we need is a start."

"Today Timbuktu," she breathed, "tomorrow the network—is that it?"

He gently nibbled her lower lip. "Uh-uh. Today, my love, we count kisses."

"I don't," she sighed over his parted lips, "precisely remember where we were."

"As I recall, you left off with the parted-lips-and—"

She interrupted to demonstrate just where she'd left off counting and decided he was, as usual, right. Kisses were indeed a better fate. . . .